THE SABBATINI BROTHERS

*Three powerful playboys
from the richest dynasty in Europe!
Ruthless, irresistible…impossible to tame?*

Luca, Giorgio and Nicoló have Italian fire and
passion coursing through their blood. And
now they are looking for the one thing that
money can't buy…the love of a good woman!

**This month Maya learns
you don't say no to Giorgio Sabbatini!**

*Hearing her say she didn't need him any more
triggered something deep and primal in his
blood. He would not let her leave him without
a fight—baby or no baby. 'You have said this
is my child, Maya,' he said. 'I am not going to
walk away from my own flesh and blood.
I have changed my mind—our marriage
will continue indefinitely.'*

**Look out for notorious Nicoló Sabbatini,
coming soon in Modern™ Romance**

Melanie Milburne says: 'I am married to a surgeon, Steve, and have two gorgeous sons, Paul and Phil. I live in Hobart, Tasmania, where I enjoy an active life as a long-distance runner and a nationally ranked top ten Master's swimmer. I also have a Master's Degree in Education, but my children totally turned me off the idea of teaching! When not running or swimming I write, and when I'm not doing all of the above I'm reading. And if someone could invent a way for me to read during a four-kilometre swim I'd be even happier!'

Recent titles by the same author:

SCANDAL: UNCLAIMED LOVE-CHILD*
THE MÉLENDEZ FORGOTTEN MARRIAGE
CASTELLANO'S MISTRESS OF REVENGE
BOUND BY THE MARCOLINI DIAMONDS

The Sabbatini Brothers

**Did you know that Melanie also writes for
Mills & Boon® Medical™ Romance?**

SHOCK: ONE-NIGHT HEIR

BY
MELANIE MILBURNE

First published in Great Britain 2010
Harlequin Mills & Boon Limited,
Eton House, 18-24 Paradise Road, Richmond, Surrey TW9 1SR

© Melanie Milburne 2010

ISBN: 978 0 263 21548 9

Harlequin Mills & Boon policy is to use papers that are natural,
renewable and recyclable products and made from wood grown in
sustainable forests. The logging and manufacturing process conform
to the legal environmental regulations of the country of origin.

Printed and bound in Great Britain
by CPI Antony Rowe, Chippenham, Wiltshire

SHOCK:
ONE-NIGHT HEIR

CHAPTER ONE

MAYA looked at the dipstick in shock. Her throat closed over as if a hand had locked around her neck as the two blue lines appeared.

Positive.

She sat on the edge of the bathtub, her legs shaking so much she had to clamp her knees together. Hope flickered brightly and then just as quickly waned.

It couldn't be true.

She took a deep breath and looked at the stick again. She blinked once, twice, three times but the lines were the same as before.

The doorbell suddenly rang with an incessant peal and she sprang to her feet, her heart knocking against her chest wall like a pendulum pushed by a madman. She quickly stashed the test kit in the nearest drawer beneath the twin basins and took a long slow breath to steady herself.

Gonzo was already at the door, barking joyfully in greeting, but Maya didn't need the dog's behaviour to signal to her who was at the door. No one rang the doorbell quite the same way as her soon-to-be ex-husband Giorgio Sabbatini did. He always pressed it too hard and for too long. He was summoning her and he clearly would not be taking no for an answer.

Maya fixed a deliberately cool expression on her face as she opened the door. 'G…Giorgio,' she said, hoping the catch in her voice wouldn't betray her. 'I thought you were sending one of your staff to pick up Gonzo. Isn't that the arrangement we agreed on?'

'I decided to come in person this time.' He bent down to ruffle the ecstatic dog's ears before he rose back to his full height, his tall frame towering over her. His dark brown eyes glittered with a sardonic light as they met hers. 'I am quite surprised to find you at home,' he said. 'I thought you might be out with your new Englishman lover. What was his name again? Hugh? Herbert?'

Maya bit the inside of her mouth, wishing, not for the first time, she hadn't gone on that stupid blind date set up by a friend from her yoga class. 'Howard,' she said tightly. 'And it wasn't anything like the press reported it.'

One of Giorgio's brows lifted in a cynical arc. 'So he didn't rip your clothes off in the hallway of his apartment and have his wicked way with you?'

Maya threw him a venomous look as she closed the door behind him with a snap. 'No,' she said. 'That is more your style, is it not?'

He gave her an indolent smile which made every hair on the back of her neck lift up in reaction. 'You were with me all the way, *cara*,' he said in a tone that was gravelly and rough and so deep she felt a guilty shiver of remembered pleasure cascade down her spine and bury itself in that hot secret place between her thighs.

Maya turned on her heel rather than face him with her colour so high. She still cringed in shame at how she had behaved the night of his brother's wedding. She still wasn't exactly sure what had precipitated it. Had it been the champagne or the pain of finally letting go? Break up sex, that was what it was called. It didn't mean anything, certainly not to him. He had probably bedded several women since they had separated. According to the latest press report, he was currently seeing a lingerie model based in London. Reading that had been like a dart to Maya's heart but she would rather die than reveal that to him.

She felt him come up behind her, her skin prickling all over and her nostrils flaring as she breathed in his citrus-based aftershave overlaid with his particular male smell. All her senses—the ones she had sworn would always be switched to neutral when he was around— turned to full throttle. She felt her heart give a stutter when his hands came to rest on the top of her shoulders, her breathing stopping altogether when his tall body brushed against hers from behind.

'You smell nice,' he said, bending his head so his mouth almost touched the side of her neck. 'Is that a new perfume you are wearing?'

Somehow she got her voice to work. 'Get your hands off me, Giorgio,' she said. *Before I turn around and fall into your arms and make a complete and utter fool of myself all over again.*

His hands tightened for a fraction of a second, long enough for her heart rate to go up another notch. 'Our divorce isn't final until the last of the paperwork is sorted,' he said, his breath lifting the hairs that had come loose from her makeshift ponytail. 'Maybe we can make the most of the time before the ink dries, hmm?'

Maya knew what this was about and it hurt much more than the lingerie model. It wasn't their broken marriage he was fighting for, it was his fortune. The Sabbatini family was as good as Italian royalty. When she had married Giorgio five years ago there had been no prenuptial agreement prepared. It was an unwritten, unspoken law: their marriage was meant to last, as every other Sabbatini marriage had in the past. But Maya wondered if any other Sabbatini marriage had endured the heartache theirs had and survived.

She very much doubted it.

She turned to face him, her heart tightening all over again as she looked into his inscrutable dark-as-night eyes. 'What do you want?' she asked.

His thumbs started to knead her knotted shoulders until she was sure she was going to melt into a pool at his feet. She fought the response, clamping her teeth together as she put her hands against his chest to push him away. 'Will you stop touching me, for God's sake?' she railed at him.

He captured her hands effortlessly, holding them in one of his as if they were a child's. 'It was good that night, *si*?' he said. 'I can't remember a time when it was better, can you?'

Maya swallowed unevenly. She had tried so hard not to think of that night, how wonderful it had been to make love with such abandon. No temperature or ovulation charts, no hormone injections—just good old-fashioned bed-wrecking sex, except they hadn't quite made it to the bed. But this visit: was it about a rerun of that passionate night or a truce to secure his assets?

'Giorgio…that night was a crazy, stupid mistake,' she said, not trusting herself to hold his gaze.

She pulled her hands out of his and moved away, crossing her arms over her middle. It was too soon to tell him, of course it was. It would jinx things just like before. How many times had she held up the dipstick in joy, only to have her hopes and dreams smashed like priceless porcelain on a pavement a week or two later? There were no guarantees this time would be any different. If it wasn't meant to be, at least Giorgio would be free to move on with someone else who could give him what he wanted most. They would both be free to move on. She had wasted five years of his life, not to mention her own. He was thirty six years old. Most of his friends and colleagues had two or three children by now.

She had given him none.

Giorgio followed her into the tiny *salone*. Maya felt his gaze on her, the heat of it, the slow burn of it peeling every layer of her skin until she felt raw and exposed. She had to hold herself together. She couldn't come unstuck and get all emotional and needy in front of him. She was supposed to be over all of that now. She had worked hard at it, working out new priorities, new directions, none of which included Giorgio. Cool and in control was the only way to go with him. She had to prove to him that he no longer had any emotional or sensual power over her. She was her own person now, determined to move on with her life.

She was stronger now, much stronger.

The six-month separation had done that for her. She no longer lived in the shadow of Giorgio's money and prestige. She was making a way for herself, providing for her future by restarting her career, which she had naively cast aside in order to fit in with what Giorgio and his family had expected of her. She was quite proud of what she had achieved in the time they had been apart. She had been looking forward to starting afresh until this latest hiccup had thrown her off course. Could he see the secret she was trying to hide from him? Was there some clue on her face or in her body, even at this early stage? He seemed to be looking at her so intently, his dark gaze so piercing she felt exposed and raw, as if he could see into her soul.

'What is this I hear about you moving to London?' he asked.

She faced him with a set mouth, her shoulders pulled back in determination. 'I have an interview for a teaching position at a fee paying school. I am on the shortlist.'

A frown brought his brows together. 'Are you going to take it if it is offered to you?'

She let her arms drop by her sides in an effort to look composed. 'I don't see why not,' she said, sending him a pointed look. 'I have nothing to keep me in Italy.'

A muscle moved up and down in his jaw, as if he were chewing on something hard and distasteful. 'What about Gonzo?' he asked.

Maya felt her heart squeeze at the thought of saying

goodbye to the dog she had brought up from puppyhood. But no pets were allowed in her apartment block in London, and she knew the big ragamuffin hound would miss Giorgio too much in any case. As it was, the dog had been like a naughty child ever since she and Giorgio had separated. 'I have decided he is better off with you,' she said.

His top lip curled. 'That's quite a turnaround. You were arguing the point for weeks over who should have him. I was about to get my lawyer to file a pet custody suit.'

Maya lifted one of her shoulders in a shrug of feigned indifference. 'I am sure he will forget all about me once he moves into your newly renovated villa,' she said. 'When do you move back in, by the way?'

Giorgio raked his hand through his hair in a gesture that tugged on something deep inside Maya's chest. There were so many of his mannerisms she had found herself thinking about lately: how he rationed his smiles as if he found life not all that amusing, how his brow furrowed when he was deep in concentration, and how his eyes glinted and darkened meaningfully when he was in the mood for sex. She skirted away from that errant thought. It brought back too many erotic memories of that forbidden night.

'I'm not sure. A week or two, I think,' he said. 'The painters haven't quite finished. There was a delay with some of the fabrics for the curtains or some such thing.'

Maya didn't want to think of how she had chosen the colours and fabrics for all of those rooms in the past. She had done it with such enthusiasm and hope for the future. When she had heard he was renovating the villa, adding rooms and knocking down walls and redeveloping the garden, she had been crushed to think he obviously wanted to rid the place of every trace of her presence. It tore her apart to think of how those rooms might one day be filled with his children by some other woman. She thought of the nursery she had so lovingly decorated the first time she had fallen pregnant. After five years of dashed hopes, in the end she had not been able to even open the door.

'When do you leave?' Giorgio asked into the pulsing silence.

With an effort she met his gaze. 'Next Monday.'

'This is all rather sudden, is it not?' he asked, frowning darkly. 'I thought you had decided long ago you weren't going to go back to teaching. Or are you trying to imply to outsiders that I'm not paying you enough in our divorce settlement?'

Maya refused to rise to the bait. 'I don't care what people think, Giorgio. I want to go back to teaching because I have a brain that longs to be used. I was never cut out for the ladies-who-do-lunch set. I should never have given up my career in the first place. I don't know what on earth I was thinking.'

He continued to study her with his dark unreadable gaze. 'You seemed pretty happy with the arrangement to begin with,' he said. 'You said your career was not as important as mine. You jumped at the chance to become a full time wife.'

Maya mentally cringed at how romantically deluded

she had been back then. Although she hadn't for a moment thought he was marrying her for love, she had longed for it to happen all the same. His marrying her had more to do with tradition and expectation from his family. He had reached the age of thirty and, in the tradition of the Sabbatini blood line, he'd needed a wife and heir. Giorgio had showered her with diamonds and she had been fooled into believing in the whole fairy tale that one day they would get their happy ever after. How young and naive she had been! Just twenty-two years old, fresh out of university, she had fallen in love on her first trip abroad. It had taken her five heartbreaking years to finally grow up and realise not all fairy tales had a happy ending.

'I had stars in my eyes,' she said, knowing it would feed his opinion of her as a gold-digger but doing it anyway. 'All that money, all that fame, all those luxury hotels and villas and exotic holidays. What girl could possibly resist?'

His brows snapped together and that leaping knot of tension appeared again at the corner of his mouth. 'If you think for even a moment that you are getting half of all I own, then think again,' he bit out. 'I don't care if it takes my legal team a decade to thrash this out in court, I will not roll over for you.'

Maya raised her chin at him. It was always about money with Giorgio. She had been yet another business transaction and the thing that rankled with him was it had failed. The truth was they had both failed. She hadn't made him any happier than he had made her. Money had cushioned things for a while but she had come to see the only way to move forward was to part.

'You will only delay the divorce even further,' she said. 'I am not after much, in any case.'

Giorgio gave a snort. 'Not much? Come on, Maya. You want the villa at Bellagio. That has been in my family for seven generations. It is priceless to my family. I suppose that's why you want to take it away from us.'

Maya steeled her resolve. 'The place should have been sold years ago and you know it. We've only been there the once and you acted like a caged lion the whole time. Both of your brothers haven't been there for months and in the whole time we've been married your mother has never once gone there. For most of the year it lies empty, apart from the staff. It's such an obscene waste.'

His eyes moved away from hers, as she knew they would. He absolutely refused to discuss the tragic event that had occurred during his childhood, and every time she had tried to draw him out over his baby sister's death he put up a wall of resistance that was impenetrable. She hated the way he always locked her out. She hated the way it made her feel as if she was not entitled to know how he felt about even the simplest things. But then all he had wanted from her was a cardboard cut-out wife, a showpiece to hang off his arm and do all the things a corporate wife was supposed to do—all the things except unlock the secret pain of his heart.

He turned his back and paced back and forth, his hands clenching and unclenching by his sides. 'My mother might one day feel the need to go back to the

villa,' he said. 'But, until she does, the place is not to
be sold.'

Maya shifted her tongue inside her cheek, still intent
on needling him. 'Are *you* planning to go there any time
soon?' she asked. 'How long's it been, Giorgio? Two or
three years, or is it four?'

He turned and faced her, his eyes blazing with something hot and hard and dangerous. 'Don't push it, Maya,'
he said. 'You are not getting the villa. Anyway, Luca
and Bronte will most probably use it now they are married. It's a perfect place for Ella to spend her childhood
holidays.'

Maya felt her insides clench as she thought of the
dark-haired, blue-eyed toddler Luca had introduced
to his family a few weeks ago. His new wife, Bronte,
a fellow Australian, had met Luca two years ago in
London, but Luca had broken off the relationship before
he had realised Bronte was carrying his child. Their
reunion and marriage had been one of the most romantic
and poignant events Maya had ever witnessed.

Being around gorgeous little Ella on the day of the
wedding had been a torturous reminder of how Maya
had failed to produce an heir. She wondered if that was
why she had acted so stupidly and recklessly once the
reception had ended. She had been so emotionally over-
wrought, so desperately lonely and sad at the break-
down of her own marriage that she had weakened when
Giorgio had suggested a nightcap.

Going back to his room at the Sabbatini hotel in
Milan where the reception was held had been her first
mistake. Her second had been to let him kiss her. And

her third…well, she was deeply ashamed of falling into his arms like that. She had acted like a slut and he had walked away from her when it was over as if he had paid for her services like a street worker.

'I want the villa, Giorgio,' she said, holding his diamond-hard gaze. 'I surely deserve some compensation. I could ask for a whole lot more and you know it.'

His jaw moved forward in an uncompromising manner, his eyes now darker than ink. 'I wouldn't want you to get the wrong idea here, Maya. I want this divorce just as much as you do. But the villa is not negotiable. I am not going to budge on this.'

His intransigence fuelled Maya's defiance, so too did his all too ready acceptance of the divorce. Surely, if he had ever felt anything for her, wouldn't he have fought to keep her by his side no matter what? The only reason he was dragging the chain a bit was over the settlement.

Her bitterness was like a hot flood inside her, scorching its way through her veins. 'You bastard,' she threw at him. 'You're rich beyond belief and you won't give me the only thing I want.'

'Why do you want it?' he asked. 'You're moving to London within days. What use would you have for a thirty-room villa?'

'I want to develop it,' she said with a combative toss of her head. 'It would make a fabulous hotel and health spa. It would provide a supplementary income to my teaching. It would be an investment, a great investment in fact.'

His eyes flashed like lightning. 'Are you deliberately

goading me?' he asked. '*Dio,* Maya, I've already warned you not to push me too far.'

'Why?' she tossed back at him. 'Are you worried you might show some human feelings for once? Some anger, some passion, or maybe even some vulnerability for a change?'

The air pulsed with a current of energy that made the skin on the back of Maya's neck start to tingle. His eyes were so black she could not tell where his pupils ended and his irises began. He had stopped clenching his hands as soon as he saw her eyes flick to them but she could sense the tension in him all the same. His face was carved from stone, his lips flat and tight. She wondered if he was going to close the distance between their bodies and take her in his arms the way he had done the night of his brother's wedding. They had argued just like this and then suddenly, instead of shouting at each other, they were locked in a passionate embrace. Her body quivered at the memory and when she met Giorgio's eyes she could almost swear he was recalling exactly the same shamelessly erotic moment when his mouth had crashed down on hers.

'Is that what you want, Maya?' he asked in a low and deep and silky tone as his hand snaked out and captured one of hers. 'You want me to lose control and take you just like the last time?'

Maya's body flared with heat, her wrist burning like a ring of fire where his fingers curled around it like a handcuff. 'You wouldn't dare,' she bit out.

He pulled her up against him, his body hot and hard and unmistakably male against her soft femininity. 'I dared before,' he reminded her. 'And you enjoyed every second of it.'

Shame flooded her cheeks but she put up her chin haughtily all the same. 'I'd had too much champagne to drink.'

His mouth turned up derisively. 'Is that the only way you can absolve yourself for sleeping with me again?' he asked. 'Come on, Maya, you were begging for it even before you had your first sip of champagne. I saw it in your eyes the moment you stepped into the church and looked at me.'

Maya remembered the moment all too well. That first glimpse of him standing there beside his brother after not seeing him for months had knocked her sideways. She had pointedly avoided him as much as possible prior to the wedding. The arrangement over Gonzo being picked up and dropped off by a neutral party had been at her insistence because she didn't trust herself in his company. Going into the church that day and seeing Giorgio, she had felt as if she were seeing him for the first time. All the bitterness and ill feeling had somehow vaporised, all she could see was a tall, commanding and handsome man with impossibly dark brown eyes which at that moment had been centred right on her. The message in his eyes had been as scorching as his touch was right now. 'Your imagination is getting as big as your ego,' she said. 'You think any woman who looks at you wants you.'

She pulled out of his hold and stepped away from him, tossing over her shoulder, 'You should probably take Gonzo with you now. His lead is hanging on the hall stand.'

'I am not going anywhere, Maya,' Giorgio said through gritted teeth.

Maya turned, trying to ignore the flutter of unease that passed through her belly at the dark glittering heat of his gaze as it meshed with hers. 'Giorgio…' She ran her tongue over her lips to moisten their sudden dryness. 'We've said all that needs to be said. The rest is in the hands of our lawyers.'

There was another beat or two of heavily charged silence.

'I didn't come here to discuss the divorce,' Giorgio said.

Maya ran her tongue over her parched lips, her stomach freefalling. 'You…you didn't?'

His eyes were unwavering on hers. 'I came here to issue you an invitation.'

She blinked at him in alarm. 'An…an invitation? What sort of invitation? I hope you don't mean what I think you mean because I will not for a moment agree to such an outrageous, insulting and indecent proposal.'

His sensually full lips went into a flat line again. 'Not that sort of invitation, not that it isn't a tempting thought, given what happened the last time.'

'It's over, Giorgio,' she said, reminding herself as well as him. '*We* are over.'

He held her look for two beats before he spoke. 'I know it's over, Maya. It's what we both want. It's what we both need to move on with our lives.'

Maya nodded because she didn't trust her voice to

work right then. Of course it was over. It was what she wanted. She was the one who had done the legwork to get the divorce process going. What sort of hypocrite was she to have second thoughts now? Even though those two blue lines on that dipstick were lying in that drawer upstairs didn't mean they would appear on a subsequent test. It could all be a mistake. She might have imagined the whole thing. She would need to do another test and another, just to make sure.

Giorgio pushed his hand back through his hair again, taking it off his forehead where it had tipped forward as he moved to the other side of the room. Maya noticed then how tired he looked about the eyes. Too much partying, she supposed. She could just imagine him enjoying the night life after years of being tied down in a going nowhere marriage. He had been like that before they had married and that, no doubt, would be his fall-back position.

'My grandfather's ninetieth birthday party is next weekend,' Giorgio said, facing her again. 'He wants you to be there.'

Maya tightened her mouth. 'Why then didn't he call and invite me, instead of sending you? Or why not send an invitation through the post? What's going on?'

'You know what he's like,' he said. 'He's a stubborn old fool who thinks we are throwing away a perfectly good marriage. He wanted me to ask you in person. He apparently thinks I still hold some sort of sway with you.' He gave her a wry look. 'I told you he was an old fool.'

Maya spun on her heel to pace the floor. 'I am *not* ·

attending any more Sabbatini family functions,' she stated firmly. 'No way. Not after the last time.'

Giorgio held up his hands. 'I promise not to touch, OK?'

She stopped mid-pace to glower at him. 'I don't hold much faith in your promises. You were barely in the door a moment ago when you put your hands on me as if you owned me.'

He gave her a crooked half smile that never failed to twist her insides. 'Put it down to force of habit or muscle memory or whatever.'

She screwed up her face in scorn. 'Muscle memory? What sort of ridiculous excuse is that? We're about to be divorced, remember? You have no right to touch me now.'

His fleeting smile disappeared and a frown pulled at his brow. 'Look, Maya, you will make an old man very happy if you agree to come. Divorce or not, he still considers you a member of the family. He will be devastated if you don't turn up.'

Maya chewed at her lip, torn between wanting to pay her respects to the only grandfather/father figure she had ever known and her reluctance to spend any further time with the one man she suspected she was not going to be able to resist if she was in too close contact with him. 'If I go it will be because *he* asked me, not you,' she said.

He jangled his keys in his pocket as if impatient to leave. *Mission accomplished*, Maya thought. He'd got what he wanted and now he was off to enjoy his freedom. She watched as he moved to the front door of her small rented villa, the words to call him back stuck like a handful of thumbtacks in her throat.

It's over.

It's what we both want.

It's over.

The words went over and over in her head like a music system stuck on replay.

'I'll pick up Gonzo the day before you leave for London,' he said as he opened the door.

'Right. Fine. OK,' Maya said, cupping her elbows to stop herself from fidgeting.

He gave her one last look, his eyes dark and unfathomable as they ran over her. 'Champagne or not, it was a great night, *cara*, wasn't it? Good note to end our relationship on.'

Maya swiftly turned her back on him, her eyes burning with unshed tears. 'Please leave…' she said, surprised her voice had come out at all, much less without cracking.

After what seemed an age, the door finally closed with a click that felt as if it had snapped her heart in two.

CHAPTER TWO

THE party for Salvatore Sabbatini was in full swing when Maya arrived the following Saturday. She had almost changed her mind about coming but knew if she didn't turn up by a certain time Giorgio would come to her place and collect her.

Right now she wanted as much distance as possible between them. Her secret was still safe and she wanted to keep it that way for as long as possible. She had conducted three more tests and they had all produced the same positive result. It was terrifyingly exciting to think she was carrying a child. Six weeks was too early to be confident it would carry to full term, but every miscarriage she'd had in the past had occurred well before the eight week mark.

'Signora Sabbatini,' one of the uniformed waiters greeted her with a tray of drinks balanced on one arm, 'would you like some champagne?'

Maya offered him a tight smile. 'Orange juice will be fine, thank you.'

Once she had taken her frosted glass, she moved through to the reception room, where a glamorous array of people were milling about to greet the guest of honour. There were Hollywood stars and high finance people, a couple of members of European royalty as well as family and close friends of Salvatore. Everyone was dressed in designer clothes and several of the women were dripping in priceless jewels.

Maya had dressed carefully for the occasion. She could play the part of haute couture-clad wife and had done so for five years. The dress she had chosen was a fuchsia pink, highlighting the natural blondness of her hair and her sun-kissed colouring from a brief holiday she had taken recently. Her heels were high, but still not high enough to bring her shoulder to shoulder to Giorgio when he appeared out of nowhere and put his hand to the small of her back.

She gave a little start and almost spilt her drink. 'What do you think you're doing sneaking up on me like that?' she said, sending him an irritated look.

'You look exquisite this evening, Maya,' he said as if she hadn't spoken. He leaned in closer and drew in a deep breath close to her neck. 'Mmm, you're wearing that new perfume again, are you not? It suits you.'

Maya scowled as she reared away from him. 'Go and mingle with your friends. Everyone will start talking if we're seen together. I don't want another press fest to deal with.'

He smiled a sinful smile, his dark eyes glinting at her. 'Let them talk. I can spend time with my soon-to-be ex-wife, can't I? Besides, we have business to discuss.'

Maya pressed her lips together. 'I haven't changed my mind about the villa. I sent the papers back to your lawyer. I am not going to let you pay me off with a lump sum. I told you what I want.'

'I know,' he said, scooping a glass of champagne off the tray of the passing waiter. He took a generous sip before he added, 'but here's the thing: I want it too.'

She looked up at him warily. 'We can't both have it, though, can we?'

His eyes locked on hers, hot and hard as steel. 'I have given it some thought. For the next twelve months I would like the villa to remain a private residence. No developments, no changes.'

She frowned. 'And after that?'

He took another sip of his champagne, his throat moving up and down slowly as he swallowed it, deliberately delaying his response, making her wait, making her feel unimportant, insignificant. 'After that, if you still want it you can buy it from my family,' he said.

Maya rolled her eyes. 'Oh, for pity's sake.'

'What's the matter, Maya?' he asked. 'I'm paying you a fortune in settlement. You'll have enough cash to buy ten villas.'

She stalked away from him. 'I don't want your stupid money.'

In an effort to move away from the interested glances aimed at her, Maya slipped out to a balcony accessed by French windows. She hadn't expected Giorgio to follow her out there but, before she could shut the doors behind her, he had stepped through them.

'Why are you being so difficult over this?' he asked, leaning back against the closed doors.

'*I* am being difficult?' she asked with an incredulous

look. 'You're the one who keeps sending legal documents the thickness of two phone books to me to sign.'

His forehead creased in a brooding frown. 'I have shareholders and investors to protect. Don't take it personally. It's just business.'

Maya put her glass of juice down on a pot stand before she dropped it. 'Oh, yes, it's always business with you. Our marriage was nothing more than a business arrangement. The only trouble was I didn't deliver the goods as promised.'

'What do you mean by that?' His voice was hard and sharp, like a flung dagger.

She dropped her gaze and let out a scratchy sigh. 'You know what I mean, Giorgio.'

A lengthy silence passed.

'I wanted it to work, Maya,' he said quietly. 'I really did, but we were both making each other miserable in the end.'

She looked up at him with a pained expression. 'You don't get it, do you?'

'What's to get?' he asked, his voice rising in frustration. 'We were married for five years, Maya. I know it wasn't easy for you. It wasn't easy for me, watching you…' He didn't finish the sentence but, moving away from the doors, lifted his glass and drained the contents.

Maya looked at his stiff spine, feeling the emotional lockout she always felt when they argued. He refused to talk about the losses they had experienced. She'd always had the feeling he had dismissed each miscarriage as nature's way of saying something was not right. She, on the other hand, had wanted to talk about each of the babies she had named as soon as they were conceived. She had wanted to talk about their stolen futures, the dreams and hopes she had had for each of them. To her, they were not a collection of damaged cells that nature had decided were best sloughed away. They had been her precious babies, each and every one of them.

Giorgio hated failure. He was a ruthlessly committed businessman who refused to tolerate defeat in any shape or form. Success drove him, as it had driven his grandfather and his late father to build the heritage that stood unrivalled in the world of luxury hotels. Giorgio had no time for life's annoying little hiccups. He wanted results and went about achieving them mercilessly if he had to. That was how Maya had ended up his wife. His father had just been injured in a terrible head-on collision and was lying in a semi-coma in hospital, not expected to live past a few weeks.

Giorgio had decided Maya would be an ideal candidate for a wife: educated, poised, young and healthy and in the prime of her reproductive life. How wrong he had been to choose her of all people, she thought bitterly. He could have done so much better, a fact some members of his family had hinted at over the last year or so. They were subtle about it, of course: an occasional comment over dinner about someone's newborn child or how one of Giorgio's school friends was now a father of twins. Each comment had been a stake through Maya's heart, worsening her sense of failure, shattering her self-confidence, destroying her hope of one day being a mother. She had failed as a Sabbatini wife. She had let the dynasty down and, until she got out of Giorgio's life, his family would continue to look upon her with pity and disappointment.

Giorgio put his glass down on the wrought iron table before he faced her. 'My grandfather is dying,' he said in a low, serious tone. 'He told me this morning. He has less than a month or two at most to live. No one else in the family knows.'

Maya felt her heart drop like a ship's anchor inside her chest. 'Oh, no...'

His throat rose and fell over a tight swallow. 'That's why he wanted all the family here tonight. He wanted tonight to be a happy celebration. He didn't want anyone's pity. He will make the announcement to family and friends in the next week or two.'

Maya could understand Salvatore's motivation in keeping tonight focused on his birthday instead of his impending demise. Pride was something she had come to recognise as a particular Sabbatini trait. Giorgio had it in buckets and barrels and spades. 'Thank you for telling me,' she said softly, not quite understanding why he had. Why hadn't he told Luca and Nic, his two brothers, for instance?

His eyes were still meshed with hers. 'I want you to think about postponing your trip to London,' he said. 'Call the school and tell them you can't make the interview. Tell them you need to take compassionate leave.'

She stared at him, open-mouthed. 'I can't take leave before I've even got the job. They will give it to someone else.'

He lifted a shoulder. 'If they do, then you weren't meant to have it. If they think you are the best one for the position they will wait until you are available.'

Maya frowned at him furiously. 'Of course they won't keep the job open for me. I'm the least experienced of the candidates. I haven't stood in front of a classroom since I was at university on teaching practice. I won't stand a chance if I don't turn up for the interview.'

'You don't need the job right at this moment, Maya,' he said. 'I have agreed on an incredibly generous allowance. If you want to work, then I am sure other jobs will come along in time.'

Maya threw him a castigating look. 'Why do you have to be so damned philosophical about everything?'

He returned her frown with a challenging arc of one brow. 'Why do you have to be so irrational and emotional?'

Maya turned away and looked out over the wintry gardens, her hands gripping the balustrade so tightly her knuckles ached. 'Is this really about your grandfather's health or an attempt to make me change my mind about the divorce?'

He didn't respond for so long she wondered if he had left her there, listening to the soft patter of the February raindrops.

'You can have your divorce, but not right now,' he said at last. 'I want my grandfather to die in peace, believing we have patched things up.'

Maya felt her heart slip like a stiletto on a slate of ice. She spun around and faced him again, her eyes wide with panic. 'You're asking me to come back and live with you as your wife?'

He held her look with enviable equanimity. 'For a month or two, that is all,' he said. 'It will make the end a lot easier for my grandfather. Our separation has upset him greatly. I had not realised how much until now.'

Maya resented the implication behind his words. 'So you're blaming *me* for his terminal illness, are you?'

His dark eyes rolled upwards in that arrogant way of his which seemed to say she was being childish and petty while he was mature and sensible. 'You are putting words into my mouth, Maya,' he said. 'My grandfather is ninety years old. It is not unexpected that he would be suffering from some sort of illness at his age. The fact that it is terminal is sad but not entirely unexpected. He has smoked rather heavily during his lifetime. He is lucky he has had as many years as he has. My father was not so blessed.'

She glared at him regardless. 'No doubt you think I have jinxed things for Salvatore or something. I announce I want a divorce and a few weeks later he is dying. I can see a pattern, even if you can't.'

A muscle twitched in the lower quadrant of his jaw. 'My father dying just a few days after we married was not your fault. It was no one's fault. It was just a tragic accident. You know that.'

'I wasn't talking about your father's death.'

His muscle moved again. 'Miscarriages are another fact of life, just like old age, Maya,' he said, barely moving his lips to speak. 'They are far more common than you think.'

Maya felt hot colour crawling beneath her skin and turned away again in case he noticed. 'If we resume living together it will only complicate and ultimately prolong our divorce,' she said after a slight pause. 'Everyone's hopes will be raised and then dashed again once we...go ahead with it in the end...'

'I realise that is something we will have to deal with,' he said. 'But, for the time being, I believe this is the best course of action.'

Maya faced him again with a lip curl of scorn. 'Why? Because it's going to give you more time to work out a way to keep your assets safe?'

He stared her down. 'You never used to be so cynical.'

She lifted her chin. 'I grew up, Giorgio. Life's repeated punches have a habit of doing that.'

He moved away to look out over the immaculate gardens as she had done moments earlier. His hands too, she noticed, were white-knuckled as he gripped not the balustrade as she had done, but the back of the wrought iron chair of the outdoor setting at least a metre away from the edge. Maya knew his fear of heights disgusted him, even though he had suffered from it since childhood. She had only found out about it by accident. He would never have told her, which said rather a lot about their relationship, she thought. He saw his fear as a weakness he had to conquer. Countless times, she had seen him fight with himself to overcome his primal reaction. His doggedness had at times both impressed her and frustrated her in equal measure. She had so often wanted to help him but he would push her away as if she had come too close, as if she would be the one to push him over the edge of the dark abyss he dreaded so much.

'I want my grandfather to die a peaceful death,' Giorgio said after a long taut silence. 'I will do anything to achieve it.'

Maya mentally ticked the box marked 'ruthless'. Giorgio would think nothing of doing whatever it took to get what he wanted, including resuming a relationship with a wife he had never loved and didn't really want now she had failed to live up to expectations, to use a particularly relevant word. He would no doubt live the lie, playing pretend while he got on with his affair with his gorgeous lingerie model.

Maya knew from experience that the press got it wrong a lot of times, but not *all* of the time. That was the thing that had plagued her the most. The 'no smoke without fire' thing had niggled at her the whole time they were married. Giorgio had always denied the occasional dalliances the press reported, but her doubts and fears had still risen to the surface like oil on water. She had waded for five years through the cloying stickiness, trying to cling to the hope that the conception and subsequent birth of a child would cement their tenuous union.

It had never happened.

She slid a hand over the flat plane of her belly, her heart giving a tight aching contraction.

It might *still* not happen...

Giorgio turned from the chair as someone came out

onto the balcony. 'Luca,' he said with a forced on-off smile. 'I didn't see you come in.'

Luca, his younger brother by two years, gave him a ready smile that lit his dark brown eyes from behind. 'We arrived late,' he said. 'Ella was a bit late having her afternoon sleep.'

He turned to Maya and bent to kiss her on both cheeks. 'It's so good you came tonight, Maya,' he said. 'Bronte will be glad of someone to talk to. She was feeling rather nervous about practising her Italian in front of everyone.'

Maya smiled shakily. 'She has no need to be,' she said. 'Everyone adores her and gorgeous little Ella.'

Luca smiled proudly. 'We have an announcement to make…' His expression faltered for a second before he continued, 'I'm sorry, this might not be the news you two want to hear, but we are expecting another baby.'

A silence thickened the air for a nanosecond.

Maya was the first to respond. 'Luca, that's truly wonderful news. I am so happy for you both. When is it due?'

'I'm not sure,' Luca said, looking a bit sheepish. 'We've only just done one of those home kit tests. It's all still a little bit unreal, to be frank.'

Tell me about it, Maya thought wryly.

Giorgio gave his brother a firm handshake, anchoring it with a grasp of Luca's forearm. 'I am very pleased for you. It will be delightful to have another niece or nephew to spoil.'

Luca appeared relieved his announcement had gone down so well. 'So,' he said, still smiling, his eyes this time full of intrigue. 'What are you two doing out here all alone?'

Another silence hovered like humidity before a storm.

Giorgio was the first to break it. 'Maya and I have an announcement of our own to make.' He put his arm around her waist and drew her into his side. 'We have decided to reconcile. There will be no divorce.'

Maya's eyes flew to his, her mouth opening but nothing coming out. The weight of his arm around her waist was like a chain, tying her to him just as effectively as his words.

Luca looked from one to the other with a spreading smile. 'That's wonderful news. Have you told *Nonno*? It will be the best birthday present for him.'

Giorgio smiled smugly. 'We are just about to do so now, aren't we, *cara*?' he said, looking down at Maya.

Maya wanted to deny it. She wanted to tell Luca his brother was a manipulating, ruthless man who would stop at nothing to keep what he wanted in his possession. But she knew if she did it would quite possibly ruin Salvatore's party. The old man was dying and Luca was right: the announcement of the reconciliation between his eldest grandson and his estranged wife would make his day.

Instead, she gave Luca a weak smile. 'It's all happened so suddenly…'

Luca grinned at his brother. 'I have to tell Bronte. She'll be so thrilled. This calls for more champagne.'

He picked up Giorgio's empty glass and then moved to where Maya had left her half-drunk orange juice. He picked it up and, after a moment, turned and looked at her quizzically. 'Not currently on the hard stuff, Maya?'

Maya felt the weight of Giorgio's gaze. 'I…I guess over the years I've got used to not drinking,' she said.

'You will have to make up for it tonight,' Luca said and, with another beaming smile, left through the French windows to find his young wife and child.

'Luca is right,' Giorgio said after what seemed an endless pause. 'This is indeed a night for celebration.'

Maya threw him a barbed glare. 'How could you lie to your own brother like that? This is a farce and you know it.'

He gave a movement of his mouth that communicated total indifference to her opinion. 'This is about making my grandfather's last weeks or months of life as comfortable and happy as possible,' he said. 'You said you wanted the villa at Bellagio.' He gave her an indomitable look and added, 'Believe me, Maya, this is the only way you are going to get it.'

CHAPTER THREE

MAYA fumed as she left the balcony with Giorgio's arm planted firmly around her waist. Even more guests had arrived and a couple of camera flashes went off. She wondered if Giorgio had primed the select members of the press present to give her no chance of denying the announcement of their reconciliation. She would look a complete and utter fool if she said anything to the contrary now. After all, she had spent the whole time so far with him out on the balcony. People had already started talking.

'Stop grinding your teeth, *mio piccolo*,' he said in an undertone as they moved through to where Salvatore was seated like a king in the main *salone*.

Maya kept her lips pressed together, her words coming out like hard pellets. 'You set this up, didn't you? You set me up so I couldn't say no. You knew I would not want to spoil your grandfather's party and you deliberately played on that.'

His arm tightened like a band of steel around her waist. It was a possessive touch but also a warning. 'Play along with it, Maya,' he said. 'Look at *Nonno*. He is enjoying himself so much. Our announcement on top of Luca and Bronte's will be the icing on the cake—literally.'

The announcement hardly needed to be made formally for as soon as they walked into the *salone* all heads turned. There were whispers and gasps, nudges and did-you-see-that looks. More camera flashes went off and then Salvatore looked directly at Giorgio and Maya and his old weathered face broke into a rapturous smile.

'Is this what I think it is, Giorgio?' he asked, tears glistening in his eyes. 'You and Maya have changed your mind about divorcing?'

Maya felt Giorgio's hand reach for hers and squeeze it gently. 'Yes, *Nonno*,' he said. 'We have called it off. We are going to work at our marriage.'

Salvatore grasped Maya's free hand and almost crushed it between both of his gnarled ones. 'Maya, you and my grandson have made me such a happy man tonight. I cannot tell you what this means to me. All my family is here around me to share this wonderful news.'

Maya could feel the bars of her gilded cage moving in on her, just as they had done for the last five years. She was trapped in a charade that went against everything she believed in. She felt such a fraud, playing to the crowd and most especially to Salvatore. She wasn't sure she could get through a night of it, let alone a few weeks. Surely someone would see it for what it was? The press were already eyeing her rather closely, she thought, or maybe that was her imagination. She had always found the intrusion of the press rather difficult to deal with. It was so different from her anonymous upbringing, when even her great-aunt had barely noticed her.

More champagne was called for and more and more cameras documented the celebration. Luca and Bronte announced their delightful news which, in Maya's mind, deserved far more attention than theirs, but it seemed everyone was intrigued by the news of the acrimonious Sabbatini divorce being called off.

Giorgio's mother greeted Maya with guarded enthusiasm. Maya understood Giovanna's caution; she had made things difficult for her son by bickering over every little detail to do with their separation, but Giovanna was gracious enough to welcome her back into the family fold. Besides, her mother-in-law was thrilled to finally be a grandmother. She doted on little Ella and, with the news of Bronte's new pregnancy, Giovanna was clearly preoccupied with the new branch of the family tree.

Nicolò, or Nic as he was more commonly called, the youngest of the Sabbatini brothers, was less accommodating. He adopted his usual sardonic expression as he approached Maya after Giorgio had gone to fetch another glass of juice for her.

'So it seems you changed your mind after reacquainting yourself with how the other half lives, eh, Maya?' he said. 'Glad you came to your senses. You weren't going to come out in front, not with Giorgio's legal team working on it.'

Maya kept her expression coolly contained, even though inside she felt furious at being reminded of how outmatched she had been right from the start. 'Hello, Nic,' she said. 'How are things with you?'

He rocked his almost empty champagne flute back and forth, his hazel eyes penetrating as they held hers. 'Fine enough,' he said.

She looked around his broad shoulders for signs of a current date. 'What? No Hollywood starlet tonight?' she asked with a mocking lift of her brows.

Nic gave her a crooked wry smile that reminded her of Giorgio in one of his rare playful moods. 'No, I didn't think *Nonno* would approve of my latest lover. He mentioned the "M" word a few moments ago. It was enough to turn me to drink.'

'You're only what…thirty-two?' she asked.

He nodded rather grimly. 'You know the Sabbatini rule. Once you turn thirty, you are meant to settle down.'

'Luca has only just done so at thirty-four,' Maya said. 'You shouldn't rush into these things. You could end up making a mistake.'

He rocked his glass again, his eyes still boring into hers. 'Like you did?'

The words hung in the air like a swinging sword.

'I don't consider my marriage to your brother to have ever been a mistake,' Maya said, wishing she really believed it. 'We just hit a rough patch, that's all.'

Giorgio came over at that moment and handed Maya a glass of juice. He must have picked up on the atmosphere, for he narrowed his gaze at his youngest brother. 'I hope you are keeping your thoughts and opinions on marriage to yourself, Nic,' he said. 'I don't want Maya upset by your teasing.'

Nic's smile was instantly charming. 'I was just

welcoming her back into the family,' he said. His expression became a little more serious as he addressed Maya directly. 'I hope it works out for you. I mean that, Maya.'

Maya wondered if he somehow sensed her insecurity. He was an out-and-out playboy—everyone knew about his wild child antics as a teenager and young adult—but the outcome of that madcap lifestyle had given him an almost intuitive sense at times. He had grown up a lot after the tragic death of his father, but it was common knowledge in the family that his mother and his grandfather in particular wanted him to settle down with a suitable wife, which was something Nic made it clear he was not prepared to do. He was a free spirit and hated being tied down. Even within the family corporation, he was the one who had been given the most flexibility. Nic was the one who travelled the world, hardly settling in one place longer than a week or two as he acquired property and oversaw the redevelopments of their hotel chain.

'Thank you, Nic,' she said. 'I aim to give it my very best shot.'

After a few more desultory exchanges with other guests and family members, Giorgio led her away to a quiet corner. He was aware of how strained she looked. Her face looked pale and he had noticed she had surreptitiously mopped at her brow a couple of times, as if she was finding it too warm. 'Don't take any notice of Nic,' he said, watching as his younger brother started chatting up a stunning redhead near the buffet table.

'Nic is Nic,' she said in a downbeat voice.

'Yes, indeed.' Giorgio sighed and looked down at Maya. 'You look tired. It's been a long night. Do you want me to take you home?'

Her fingers slipped on the glass she was holding and he took it from her before she dropped it. 'Sorry,' she said, glancing up at him self-consciously before looking away again, her teeth sinking into her bottom lip.

He studied her for a moment, wondering if he should have given her more warning about his intentions. Dropping it on her like that out on the balcony had obviously shocked her. But he was still reeling himself from his grandfather's revelation. Salvatore had always seemed so ageless to Giorgio. In spite of his weathered skin and arthritic body, his mind was sharp and he still had an active role in the corporation. Giorgio felt humbled by the trust his grandfather had shown in him by telling him first about his illness. Ever since the death of Giorgio's father, Giancarlo, Salvatore had entrusted more and more responsibility on Giorgio's shoulders. It would be very hard to say that final goodbye to the man who was not just his grandfather but his business partner and friend.

Maya too would find it hard. She had developed a special kind of relationship with Salvatore over the five years of their marriage. She had grown up in a single parent household but then tragically, when she was just ten years old, her mother had been killed in an accident. Maya had been brought up by a great-aunt who had never married and had no children of her own. Maya hadn't spoken much about her childhood. She seemed to find it painful so Giorgio mostly had avoided the topic.

He had been delighted when Maya had expressed her avid desire to have children. It was one of the things that made him so determined she was the one he should marry. When the first couple of pregnancies had ended in a miscarriage he had been upset, but out of concern for Maya he had concealed his feelings. He hadn't wanted her to think she had let him down. He knew she had blamed herself, wondering if there was something wrong with her for not being able to have a child. It was only after the fourth miscarriage had occurred that he wondered if somehow it was him that was causing the trouble. But subsequent tests had shown that he was fine, although sometimes he still worried.

And then Maya had stopped falling pregnant altogether. They had done everything they were told to do. They kept temperature charts, Maya mapped her ovulation period and they had sex when she was supposedly most fertile, but still she'd failed to conceive.

The progression to IVF was something he had not felt entirely comfortable with. It all seemed so clinical, nothing like the sex they used to have when they'd first met. Nothing like the sex they had the night of Luca and Bronte's wedding.

His body tightened as he recalled that night. He hadn't cared about anything other than having her as quickly and as passionately as he could. It had been the best sex of his life and he wanted more. He had realised that the day he had gone to her flat to invite her to the party. He had gone there thinking their one-night stand would have cooled his ardour. He had been confident he could have seen her, talked to her and even touched her without feeling a thing. He had been shocked to find out how wrong he was. Putting his hands on her shoulders had sent zapping wires of electric want through him. He wanted Maya as he wanted no other woman. How could he have forgotten how fantastic it was with her? His body had tingled for hours afterwards. He only had to look at her and his blood raced through his veins and made him rock-hard.

He was feeling it now, standing so close to her, breathing in her sexy new fragrance: flowery but spicy and exotic at the same time. The dress she was wearing brought out the glow of her skin and the platinum blond of her hair. She had left it loose this evening, the way he most liked it. Before he even realised he was doing it, he reached out and threaded his fingers through the silk of it where it lay about her shoulders.

She gave a little shudder of reaction and looked up at him. 'Do you have to do that?' she asked in an undertone.

'We are supposed to be reconciled, *cara*,' he said, taking the opportunity to brush his lips against her forehead. 'People will expect us to touch each other in public. They will imagine we will be doing much more when we are finally at home alone.'

'Where is home supposed to be now?' she asked in a soft breathless sort of voice. 'Your place or mine?'

Giorgio shifted his mouth ruefully as he straightened. 'My place, or what used to be our place, is not quite ready. I've been staying at the hotel most nights. We will have to stay at yours tonight, otherwise the press will not believe we are truly reunited.'

'You think they will follow to check up on us?' she asked with a worried frown.

He gave her a wry look. 'Surely you haven't forgotten what the press is like. Haven't they been on your tail over the last six months of our separation?'

Maya captured her lip between her teeth, thinking of all the times she'd had to get away from the intrusive eyes of the press. That ridiculous 'date' with Howard Herrington was a case in point. They had blown it right out of proportion with a photograph that looked far more intimate than it was. She had been leaning forward, trying to catch something Howard had been saying and a flashbulb had captured the moment, making it appear she was about to press a kiss close to Howard's mouth. When it appeared in the gossip pages the following day she had taken a devil-may-care approach to the fallout. There had been a photo only a week earlier of Giorgio with his model friend. It seemed fitting that Maya had started to reclaim her life, even if Howard Herrington was the worst date she had ever had.

Maya cast her eyes over the crowd. The party was in full swing now; several couples were dancing as the band played some classic dance hits. She remembered the days when she had danced in Giorgio's arms; he had swung her around and around and even though her head had been left spinning she had always gone back for more. The early days of their courtship and marriage had been so much fun, so dizzyingly exciting for a girl who had grown up with so little. There had been no parties that she could remember during her childhood, no massive family gatherings, no huge celebrations of her own or anyone else's milestones or achievements.

As soon as she had met Giorgio she had clung to him and his family, subconsciously looking for the anchor she had lacked for much of her life. She had slotted in like a small sea-tossed craft into a safe and sheltered harbour.

She had never wanted to be cast adrift.

She had done that herself.

But now the rules had been changed. She was back, but only temporarily. Giorgio wanted her to pretend things were back to normal and she could do that for a few weeks, maybe even a month or two. The chances were her pregnancy would disappear down the drain of despair, just like the others had done. All she had to do was keep it a secret until Giorgio's game of pretend was over. There was no point in getting his hopes up as well as hers, or anyone else's for that matter.

Maya's heart ached at the thought of Salvatore dying. He was such a vitally alive man. He was the last of the great patriarchs. He liked the authority his position warranted as the elder of the tribe. She had learned a lot watching the family dynamics over the past five years. The meshing of different personalities, the way each son was cast from the same mould but still so very different. Giorgio was more like his grandfather than anyone. She suspected that was why Salvatore had told him about his illness first. Salvatore knew Giorgio would have the strength to carry the rest of the family through such a difficult time. He would watch over the family finances, he would steer a steady course instead of wavering about in panic. He would grieve certainly, but in private. He would not need anyone to support him.

He never had.

Giorgio led her to say their goodbyes to his grandfather and his mother. There were more congratulatory comments, more camera flashes and an even bigger smile from Salvatore as he gripped his eldest grandson's hand in his. 'You have made me a very happy man, Giorgio. I hoped and prayed you would not give up on your marriage. I knew you would win her back once you put your mind to it.'

Maya stretched her lips into a smile as Salvatore turned his attention to her.

'Maya, you are good for my grandson. You bring out the human, more softer side of him. Don't give up on him, *mio piccolo*. You remind me of my adored wife, Maria. She was so strong, even though like you she looked so petite and fragile. Just like her, you have backbone. I knew it from the first moment I met you.'

'I hope you enjoy the rest of your party,' Maya said, leaning forward to kiss him on both cheeks. She brushed at the tears that had sprung from her eyes and added, 'I love you.'

Salvatore smiled indulgently as she stood back with Giorgio's arm looping around her waist. 'I have never doubted it,' he said. 'Now, go home with your husband and convince him of the same.'

CHAPTER FOUR

'WE CAN'T possibly live together in this small flat,' Maya said as she opened the villa door a short time later.

Gonzo was bouncing up and down, his tail going like a metronome on twelve eight time, not unlike the rate of Maya's heartbeat.

Giorgio closed the door after waving off a car that had tailed the limousine that had brought them home. He turned and scratched behind Gonzo's ears before straightening to face her. 'Why not?' he asked. 'It has a bed, does it not?'

Maya felt her stomach flip over. 'Y…yes, but only the one.'

He gave an up and down lift of his brows that sent another shockwave through her belly. 'Then we will have to share it.'

She took a step backwards, her hands going up to ward him off. 'No way,' she said. 'There is no way I am sharing my bed with you. You can sleep on the sofa.'

He glanced at the cheap sofa she had picked up in a second-hand sale in one of her staunch attempts to move away from the wealth he took for granted, having had it all of his life. His lip curled in disdain, as she knew it would. 'I wouldn't let Gonzo sleep on that,' he said. 'Anyway, how do you expect to fit the whole six foot four of me on that thing?'

Maya gave her head a little toss and began to move away. 'Not my problem.'

One of his hands captured her like a cobra striking out at its prey. One minute she was free, the next she was standing up against the hard wall of his body, his dark eyes burning like embers as they held hers. 'I think you might have missed something in our conversation earlier, Maya,' he said in a deep silky voice. 'This reconciliation of ours is not just a show for the press.'

Maya felt her eyes widen and her heart gave another uncoordinated sprint. 'What do you mean?' She swallowed a tight knot of panic in her throat. 'You surely don't want to…to…' She swallowed again when she saw the way his eyes darkened even further.

Oh, dear God, he did.

One of his hands began stroking the length of her forearm, back and forth in a mesmerising movement that was loaded with erotic sensuality. Her skin leapt at his touch, her spine went to water and her inner core contracted as if he were already driving through her hot moistness to brand her as his.

'We might as well make the most of the situation,' he said into the throbbing silence. 'What do you say? Shall we see if we can still do it like we did the night of Luca and Bronte's wedding?'

Maya tried to pull out of his hold but it was like trying to disengage from a steel trap. 'Th…this is not what I agreed to…' she said, trying to keep her voice steady and controlled. 'I thought we were just acting, you know… out in public. Not in private. Not when we're alone.'

His fingers had found her pulse at her wrist and his caress slowed to a drugging pace that made her brain turn the rational and sensible switch to irrational and impulsive. She was in danger of betraying everything she had worked so hard over the last six months to achieve: independence, confidence and immunity. She wasn't immune and that was the biggest shock of all. She had never quite got there in terms of invulnerability and quite possibly never would. He only had to look at her in that brooding all male way of his and she felt her whole body turn into a wanton needy mess.

He pulled her even closer against him, letting her feel the heat of his arousal. 'You know we could never share a flat or villa, no matter how big or small, without it coming to this,' he said in that spine-tingling gravel-rough tone he always used when he wanted sex. Not pre-planned sex, not sex with a jar or to a meticulous timetable, but sex when everything that their bodies wanted and craved was paramount.

Like at his brother's wedding.

Like now…

Maya had to scramble mentally to regain lost ground. She was in a vulnerable period of this surprise pregnancy. All the medical advice she had received in the past was no sex until the three-month mark, just to be safe. Not that she had ever got there—the three-month mark, that was. Giorgio had been so good about it—perhaps *too* good about it. It had often made her wonder if he had simply taken his needs elsewhere when she had been unavailable. Maya knew about his father's well documented affairs in the early years of his marriage to Giovanna. Of course, since his untimely death he had been enshrined as a saint but, according to what Maya had heard, he had been anything but. Was it a case of like father like son? Luca was a bit of an unknown to her, but Nic was certainly everything a playboy should be, just as Giorgio had been before they had married.

'I don't want to sleep with you, Giorgio,' Maya said with as much firmness as she could muster. It wasn't much: a bit like a Chihuahua trying to round up a herd of wildebeest, she thought.

'You know you don't mean that,' he said, his warm coffee-scented breath caressing her face just as sensually as his thumb was now doing over her leaping pulse.

'I...I do,' she said, gulping over another tight swallow.

His expression hardened, as if his blood supply had suddenly released a shot of cynicism into his veins. 'Herbert wouldn't approve of a bit of ex-sex?' he taunted.

Maya cringed all over again at how stupid she had been to use that poor lonely man as a payback for Giorgio's sexual exploits. 'Howard,' she said through gritted teeth. 'His name is Howard and I didn't sleep with him.'

Giorgio laughed but his thumb didn't stop on her wrist. 'Poor Howard. He probably didn't get much time for sleeping. Not with you in his bed.'

Maya glared at him. 'What about your lingerie

model? Did you manage to get any sleep while you were with her?'

'I did, actually,' he said, bending down to nibble at one of her ears. 'She bored me to tears.'

Maya angled her head away, arching so much she felt a pain in her back and, before she could stop it, let out a little sharp cry. 'Ow!'

Giorgio released his hold, just using his hands to keep her upright. '*Cara*, what's wrong? Did I hurt you?' he asked, frowning with dark seriousness.

She shook her head and eased out of his loose hold, rubbing at her lower back. 'It's nothing,' she said, not quite meeting his eyes. 'I think I may have overstretched myself in my yoga class.'

'Let me massage it for you,' he offered.

Oh, no, Maya thought. That would be asking for more trouble than she needed right now. 'I'm fine, really. I just need a hot bath or something.'

'Where's the bathroom?' he said. 'I'll run it for you.'

Maya looked at him with suspicion. 'What's with the loving husband routine?' she asked. 'No one's watching, Giorgio. There are no paparazzi cameras peering through the windows.' *Thank God*, she added mentally.

His mouth tightened around the edges. 'Must you always misread my motives? I am merely doing what I would do for anyone.'

Maya gave him a scornful look. 'Oh, yes, anyone you were trying to seduce into your bed, that is.'

He muttered something under his breath that sounded

very much like a very rude word but she didn't stay around to confirm it. She stalked through to the kitchen, opening and then banging the cupboard door shut as she got out a glass for water. She turned on the tap and filled the glass and, once it was full, turned and leaned back against the sink to steady her shaking legs.

Giorgio followed her into the room which, prior to this moment, had seemed of a reasonable size. Now, with him standing there within touching distance, Maya instantly downgraded it to a kitchenette.

'You sound jealous, Maya,' he said, leaning against the opposite counter, his feet crossed over at the ankles in an indolent manner.

Maya drained her glass and set it on the sink with a little clatter. 'Why should I be jealous?' she asked. 'We were officially separated for six months. We were both free agents. You could sleep with whomever you liked. So could I.'

Her answer appeared to annoy him, as that tiny hammer of tension began beating beneath the skin at the edge of his mouth. 'Exactly how many times did you see this Hugh?' he asked.

'Howard.' Maya rolled her eyes in annoyance. 'H.O.W.A.R.D. Howard.'

'You didn't answer my question.'

'And I am not going to,' she said, pushing herself away from the sink. 'Firstly, it's none of your business and, secondly, I don't want all the details of who you've been seeing, that is, of course, assuming you haven't lost count by now.'

'You, of all people, should know you can't take what is written in the press as gospel,' he said.

She gave him an ironic arch of her brows. 'Funny that you don't adhere to your own philosophy on that issue, isn't it? But then, there is always one rule for you and another one for everyone else.'

'Maya, this is getting us nowhere,' he said, uncrossing his ankles and straightening. He expelled his breath on a sigh and sent one of his hands through his hair. 'You are exhausted. You look as if a sneeze from me would send you through that wall there to the next room. Why don't you go to bed? I will make do on the sofa.'

Maya hesitated. He would not get a wink of sleep on that sofa and they both knew it. Why he was being so chivalrous about it was beyond her. The old Giorgio would have had her flat on her back by now, sending her to paradise for the second, if not the third or fourth, time. Just thinking about it brought hot colour to her cheeks. Her body was so aware of him; each time he moved, another part of her would register it and respond. How she wanted to close that small distance between them and throw herself into his arms, begging him to take her back, to love her, even if she couldn't ever provide him with an heir. But that small distance of a few cracked and faded tiles might as well have been a canyon.

'It's just for tonight,' Giorgio said. 'I don't think I could bear any longer than that in this dump. What were you thinking, renting something like this?'

Maya folded her arms and looked at him drolly. 'I am surprised you can speak so clearly with all those silver spoons sticking out of your mouth.'

He laughed again, but this time it wasn't mocking like before. It was the sort of laugh she had heard so rarely from him over the past five years. The sort of laugh that made her spine fizz, as if a fairy was tiptoeing its way over each of her vertebrae to dance amongst the tiny hairs at the back of her neck.

'Maya,' he said, his expression suddenly turning serious once more, 'I know the difference in our upbringings has always been an issue for you. I can do nothing to change that. It is just what is. You should be grateful I can provide for you. So many women suffer financially as a result of a divorce. Once our marriage is finally over you will be richer than you could ever have been as a teacher, even if you ended up at the top of the academic ladder.'

Maya felt her heart sink at the when-not-if approach he was taking to the divorce. She knew she only had herself to blame—she had been the one to instigate the separation, but still...

He closed the distance before she could move away, his hand coming down on the top of one of her shoulders before moving to the sensitive nape of her neck. 'Tomorrow we will move back into my villa,' he said. 'It doesn't matter if the curtains are not quite finished and the paint not quite dry. At least we will have more space and privacy there.'

Maya tried not to be affected by his touch but it was impossible to ignore the way her body was automatically leaning towards him like a compass point. How long before she would betray herself all over again? If he kissed her now it would be so hard to resist him. Her lips ached for the press of his. She had to bit her tongue to stop it sweeping out to deposit a layer of moisture to them in case he saw how much she wanted him to reach for her.

'What about the household staff?' she asked, thinking of the veritable droves of people who hovered about, waiting upon every need. It was yet another one of the things that had driven her crazy towards the end. The constant speculative glances at her belly and then the raised brows whenever she and Giorgio exchanged a few heated words, as any normal married couple did at times. The trouble was, they hadn't lived a normal married life. They had lived in a fish bowl—a very expensive fish bowl that, over five years, had become an oversized, overstaffed, overstocked aquarium.

Giorgio's hand dropped from her nape and he thrust it, along with his other one, into his trouser pocket. 'I have simplified my life a bit,' he said. 'I took on board what you said in one of our arguments towards the end. The villa was starting to feel more like a Sabbatini hotel than a home. I had grown up with servants so it seemed normal to me, but I can see now how you would find it intrusive. After all, you spent far more time there than me, due to my work commitments.'

Maya could barely believe her ears. She looked at him for a long moment, her forehead wrinkling as she thought about how his life would surely soon slip back into   billionaire-with-everyone-at-his-beck-and-call mode.

He smiled crookedly. 'You don't believe me, do you,

cara? What's the problem? Can't you picture me doing my own cooking?'

'I can see you doing the celebrity chef thing in the kitchen,' she said. 'But, as for pushing a vacuum cleaner or a mop about the place, not to mention doing the laundry, well, no, quite frankly, I can't.'

'I haven't quite offloaded all the housework,' he said with a lingering smile. 'But Carita, my new housekeeper, only comes in twice a week and only for half a day.'

'Is she young and beautiful?' Maya asked, mentally picturing a lingerie model clone flouncing around the villa, wearing nothing but a pair of high heeled fluffy mules and carrying a pink feather duster in her perfectly manicured hand.

Giorgio took one of his hands out of his pocket and traced a barely touching caress down the curve of her cherry-red cheek, his gaze dark and intense as it held hers. 'You really are jealous, aren't you?'

Maya put up her chin but she couldn't quite bring herself to move away from his touch. 'Maybe, but then so are you. You keep harping on about Howard as if I was about to marry him as soon as our divorce is final.'

A flicker of something dark and dangerous moved behind his gaze. The ensuing silence was tense and unbroken for long pulsing seconds that to Maya felt like years.

But then, just as suddenly, it was over.

'Are you thinking of marrying again?' he asked as he stepped back from her.

'I haven't thought much about it,' she said and, taking a painful breath, added, 'What about you?'

He looked at her and then looked away again. 'There is not the same pressure on me now that Luc and Bronte have settled here with Ella and their future child. When our divorce is final I will have more time to think about what I want in terms of a relationship, or even if I want one at all.'

'So you won't be marrying for the sake of convenience next time around, I take it?' she asked with an arch look.

'It was convenient for both of us, Maya,' he said as a frown settled between his brows. 'I gave you everything I could. You wanted for nothing. I made sure of it. Our relationship ran its course. There was nothing either of us could do about it.'

You could have loved me, Maya thought. *Then maybe our relationship would have had a chance.*

Giorgio drew in a deep breath and slowly released it. 'I need to get some sleep and so do you. You wouldn't happen to have a spare toothbrush, would you? I didn't think to pack anything.'

'I think there's one in one of the bathroom basin drawers,' she said. 'There are fresh towels on the rail.'

Giorgio moved past her and went up the narrow staircase, stooping as the steps changed direction halfway up. The bathroom made him feel like a giant. He had to bend almost double to examine his reflection in the mirror. He looked every bit as tired as Maya looked, he thought. And, yes, she was right: he was every bit as jealous, if not more so. He hadn't even slept with that airheaded lingerie girl, not that she hadn't been keen. The opportunity had been there but he hadn't taken it.

He had sent her on her way and downed half a bottle of whisky instead.

He breathed out a sigh, not really wanting to think about that particular headache, and opened the drawer beneath the basin. It was filled with the usual female bathroom paraphernalia: cotton tips, tweezers, tampons, tissues and a brand new toothbrush, still in its packet.

And then his eyes zeroed in on something else...

CHAPTER FIVE

MAYA was making up the sofa as best she could with a spare blanket and a pillow when she sensed rather than heard Giorgio come in. The hairs on the back of her neck rose and even Gonzo dropped to his belly and gave a little doggy whimper, just like he did when a particularly nasty storm was approaching.

'Maya.'

She turned from smoothing out the blanket and came face to face with Giorgio's thunderous expression. Her eyes flared in panic when she saw what was in his right hand. Her heart knocked against her ribcage as if someone had shoved it from behind and her mouth went completely dry, so dry she had to brush her tongue out over her lips. 'I…You weren't supposed to find that…' *God, how awful that sounded*, she thought in anguish.

He put the positive dipstick down with careful precision on the small coffee table near the sofa. It was like laying down a challenge. It lay in the space between them accusingly, threateningly, dividing them, Maya thought, when it should have been uniting them.

'When were you going to tell me about this?' he asked with diamond-hard eyes.

She sent the tip of her tongue out again to loosen her lips enough to speak. 'I…I didn't think it was worth telling you because—'

'Because it's not mine?' He cut her off savagely.

Maya's mouth dropped open. She couldn't speak for the shockwave of hurt that smashed over her. She shuddered with it. She even felt as if she would collapse with it. Bright lights like thousands of silverfish darted in front of her eyes and she had to grasp the end of the sofa to steady herself. His reaction was something she had not expected—not even for a moment had she anticipated such a response from him. How could he think that of her? But then she recalled the way the press had handled her one date since their breakup. Of course he would automatically assume the child was not his. After all, they had been unable to conceive for years. It would be all too easy to assume someone else had got her pregnant. She bit her lip as she thought about things from Giorgio's perspective. She felt ashamed that her focus had always been on how *she* felt about not getting or staying pregnant. She hadn't really asked him what he felt about it. Had he felt less of a man? Had he felt less potent, less virile because he hadn't been able to fulfil what he saw as one of his primary roles as a husband?

Giorgio swung away and paced the room, or at least with what little space allowed for his long legs. He stopped after a moment and faced her, his expression so full of loathing Maya actually cringed. 'Were you hoping to pass it off as mine?' he asked. 'Was that what that night was all about after my brother's wedding? You know, I did think at the time how it was a little out of character for you. You were the one so insistent on a divorce and then there you were, tearing my clothes off.'

'I didn't tear your clothes off.' It wasn't much of a comeback or a defence but it was all Maya could think of at the time. 'We were both almost fully dressed apart from…you know…'

Giorgio sent her a livid glare. 'No, you didn't bother with the preliminaries. It was all about getting laid as quickly and as thoroughly as possible so you could get your insurance policy in place.'

Maya wrung her hands for the want of something better to do. 'It wasn't like that, Giorgio…'

'Damn it; what was it like?' he demanded furiously.

It was wonderful, it was just like the old times and it was spontaneous and passionate and totally unforgettable, but she couldn't tell him that. 'I never intended sleeping with you that night,' she said. 'The thought never crossed my mind.' *Liar,* her conscience prodded her. It was just as he had said the other day. She had thought of nothing else from the moment she had walked into the church and seen him standing next to his brother. It had reminded her so much of their wedding, how excited she had been, how gorgeously handsome Giorgio had looked and how she had been so proud to be his chosen wife, even if he hadn't once openly declared he loved her.

No wonder she had consumed one too many glasses of champagne at his brother's reception. No wonder she had been so unguarded when he'd suggested they go up to his room to discuss the terms of the divorce. What a silly fool she had been. He had set the scene for seduction, not her. How ironic that he had twisted things round to blame her for the consequences.

Giorgio stabbed a finger at her. 'You are a calculating little gold-digger,' he said. 'I am not the fool you take me for. How could this child possibly be mine when for two and a half years I have not been able to get you pregnant?' He changed the stabbing motion to a numerical one. '*Two and a half years*, Maya.' He underlined the words with his biting tone. 'Do you know how many times we had sex during that time?'

Maya was close to tears but pride would not allow her to give in to them. 'You are the father, Giorgio, but my advice is to enjoy it while it lasts because it might not last much longer.'

His throat moved up and down as if he was trying to swallow a boulder. 'What are you saying?'

She met his frowning gaze with her glistening one. 'I am six weeks pregnant. I have never gone past eight weeks, you know that. Most doctors say twelve weeks is the time to stop holding your breath; others say fourteen.'

Six weeks. Giorgio did the maths in his head. He wasn't the financial controller of the Sabbatini Corporation for nothing. His stomach clenched as if a cruel pair of sharp-edged tongs had snatched at his insides.

Six weeks.

One thousand and eight hours ago.

The night of Luca and Bronte's wedding, the night

when he had lost all control and taken Maya like a whore, not even bothering to make sure she got home safely. He had sent her on her way without a word. Pride had kept him silent. He hadn't wanted to beg her to stay the night, to stay another night and the night after that. But he had sent her away because that was what she had wanted. Damn it, it was what they had both wanted. They'd been desperately unhappy, sniping at each other at every turn. Sure, she was the one who'd insisted on bringing an end to their marriage, but it would only have been a matter of time when he would have got around to it.

But, if they were expecting a child, how could he possibly agree to a divorce now? He had been stalling over the divorce, making things as difficult for her as possible, not just because of what he stood to lose financially, although, as financial controller of a large corporation, he could not discount it. It was the sense of defeat he hated. He had failed to keep his marriage on track. He had failed to give her a child, the child they both desperately wanted. Their marriage had died and he hadn't been able to stop it. He had a list of excuses, which were all valid in their own way: the death of his father, the added responsibility that had put on his shoulders and then the fertility problems he and Maya had encountered. All had conspired against him to bring him to this impasse. Maya was on one side, wanting what she could get before she got out of his life for good, and he was on the other, wondering if there was anything he could have done differently.

The first thing he had to do was retract his appallingly

cruel accusation. What was he thinking, accusing her of such behaviour when she had never shown any sign of it in the past? For the whole time they were married she had been faithful, even in the face of the scurrilous rumours that from time to time circulated around him when he travelled. It was the one thing he admired about her, the way her moral code was so unlike those of many of her peers. He had been her first lover and he had never forgotten how precious that moment had been for them both.

He cleared his throat, feeling like a schoolboy instead of a thirty-six-year-old man in charge of a billion euro corporation. 'Maya,' he began, 'I don't know how to say this but I want—'

The flash of her grey eyes cut him off mid-sentence. 'I am not consenting to a paternity test. Not until after the birth, if there is one. It's too risky.'

Giorgio felt another dagger point of guilt slice at his gut. 'I am not asking for a paternity test.'

'Y…you're not?' Her wary look wounded him all over again.

'No,' he said. 'If you say the child is mine, then it is mine. The timing is spot on, in any case. And I didn't use any protection. It has to be my child.'

She turned away in disgust. 'So what you're really saying is if there was any doubt over the time frame you would be marching me off to some laboratory for a test.' She threw him a contemptuous look over her shoulder. 'God, you're such a heartless bastard, Giorgio.'

Giorgio took that direct hit because he knew he deserved it. Over the last six months of their bitter

separation he had started to see a side to Maya he had
not realised she had possessed. She was a lot feistier than
he had accounted for previously. She had always seemed
so demure, so acquiescent, and yet over the time of their
drawn-out estrangement he had seen her toughen up and
fight back in a way that he found strangely arousing.

'It was a shock to find the test like that,' he said.
'You know I don't like surprises. I didn't have the time
to think it through.'

He pushed his hair back from his forehead, reminding himself he needed to get it cut. Maya used to do
it for him once. When had she stopped? He couldn't
quite remember. He used to love the feel of her fingers
running through his hair as she snipped away at it. She
had chatted to him as she went about her task, giggling
at his dry asides until the haircut inevitably turned into
something else entirely.

But that was back in the early days…

She turned around to face him but her stance was de-
fensive. Her arms were across her middle but he couldn't
stop his eyes dropping to her still flat belly. The thought
of his seed growing there, their combined cells rapidly
dividing, the promise of new life so fragile and yet so
hopeful, he felt a tight ache in his chest. *Please let this
one survive*, he prayed to the God he had neglected and
ignored for most of his adult life. He wanted to reach
out and lay his hand across that precious part of Maya's
anatomy, to ensure his child's safety, to protect it with
the promise of his love throughout its life, no matter
how short or long. *Please*, he begged.

'I don't want the press to find out about this,' Maya

said. 'I don't think I could cope with everyone speculating on whether I will last the distance with this one.'

Giorgio understood what she was saying. He was used to the press, or as used to the press as anyone living in the limelight could be. He had grown up with the comments and the fabrications and the almost but not quite truths, but Maya had grown up in an entirely different world. She had been anonymous in her small suburb, and then the city of Sydney, where she had studied before travelling abroad. She had never got used to people recognising her, stopping her in the street for a comment or a photograph. Almost from the start she had shrunk in on herself, as if she wanted to hide from the world. He could see that now, when it was almost too late to change things.

Why hadn't he protected her more? Prepared her more? He had taken so much for granted: that she would slot into his high profile life as if she was born to it. By marrying her, he had cast her into a world totally foreign to her: a world of dog-eat-dog, where people took advantage of each other for financial gain, for a higher step on the social ladder. Maya had done her best to fit in, she had played the game as best she could, but it had come at a price.

Since she had left him, it had made him see his own life in retrospect. He had not had time to properly grieve the sudden loss of his father. He was still haunted by the tragic loss of his three-month-old baby sister all those years ago. Giorgio had always known the pressure to produce an heir had come from the devastating loss his parents had experienced. They had subconsciously, or perhaps even consciously, wanted to replace the tiny daughter they had lost so unexpectedly. Neither of them had returned to the villa at Bellagio since. It lay empty, as Maya had pointed out, for most of the year. No one spoke of it. It was too painful for Giorgio's mother, especially since his father had died. Giorgio knew he should have told Maya more about that time but he too had locked it away. The one time he had taken her there, at her insistence, he had felt on edge the whole time. It had been too hard to confront his feelings about the place where he had left his childhood and innocence behind.

'I will do what I can to keep the press from knowing about this for the time being,' he said. 'But it might not be something I can fully control. Have you seen a doctor yet?'

She pressed her lips together for a moment. 'No, not yet.' She looked up at him like a lost child looking for directions. 'I wasn't sure whether to believe the test or not. I thought I might wait a week or two more…you know…to be absolutely sure…'

Giorgio knew what she was waiting for and it struck him again how misguidedly he had handled things in the past. He had allowed her to think he viewed her early miscarriages as blips in nature's course, hoping that by outwardly taking a philosophical approach it would help her get over it without the added burden of his own sense of failure and loss. He knew how much she had emotionally invested in each of them. He had done the same. Why hadn't he told her how he felt? Maybe it would have helped her cope if he had shared the loss instead of pretending it was nothing to worry about. Each one of those pregnancies had had the potential to be a child.

Their child.

After seeing his parents go through the loss of his baby sister, he had closed the door on his feelings. It had been the only way he had coped. But it had left him seriously short-changed.

Maya had from the moment she had fallen pregnant been planning each child's graduation and wedding while he had said nothing. No wonder she thought him a heartless unfeeling bastard.

'You need to get it properly confirmed for a start,' he said. 'We will have to trust the doctor's confidentiality on that but I am sure that won't be a problem. You will need to rest as much as possible. Are you feeling well in yourself?'

She bit into her bottom lip again, reminding him once more of a small child abandoned by what it held most secure. 'I'm a bit nauseous but not overly so. I am tired on and off, and I have a bit of a backache, but I think that is more to do with overdoing it, as I said, at yoga.'

'I think you should stop all formal exercise until you have clearance from the doctor,' he said. 'You have to take it easy, Maya. This is the most important event in your life. We've been given a second chance. Don't do anything to compromise it.'

Her grey eyes moved out of the range of his. 'Don't fuss over me, Giorgio. It won't change anything. If I lose this baby…' she gulped as if the words had hurt as she said them '…I don't want to get my hopes up too soon…'

Giorgio came over and enveloped her in his arms. It felt so good to hold her close. She fitted into his frame like a key going into a complicated lock. He buried his head into the blond silk of her hair, breathing in the scent of gardenia and the delicate feminine fragrance that was hers alone.

He could never forget it. It had lived on his skin for months.

Six months.

'Try not to worry, *cara*,' he said, already doing the worrying for her. 'What will be will be. We have no control over this. All we can do is take the necessary precautions to ensure this pregnancy gets the best chance possible to survive.'

She raised her pain-filled eyes to his. 'And if it doesn't?'

How could he answer? He wanted what she wanted. He wanted an heir, a child of his own, with his blood flowing through its veins. He had never doubted he would get what he wanted until they had encountered all those hurdles. Like so many people, he had readily, naively assumed he would do the deed and get the results he wanted.

Life, with its twists and turns, had a way of making you re-evaluate that assumption. He took very little for granted these days. He lived from moment to moment, wondering if he would achieve the things he most wanted in life. His work fulfilled him, it challenged him enough to satisfy him, but it wasn't enough. It wasn't nearly enough. He wanted what Luca had. Luca hadn't had it easy; there was no way Giorgio could say any different. Luca had suffered, but he had come through. He had a beautiful loving wife and a gorgeous little daughter and another child on the way. What more could any man want?

It was what Giorgio wanted but, if he couldn't have it, surely that was in the lap of the gods, out of his control. That didn't sit well with him, however. He liked control. He was used to control. He controlled everything that needed controlling. He did the numbers, he aligned the figures, he knew what had to be done and he did it.

But sometimes it just wasn't enough.

'Maya,' he said, struggling to find the right words, 'if this doesn't work out, if you still want a divorce at the end, we will discuss it then and only then. We are only together now for my grandfather. The pregnancy is a bonus, a surprise package that we can only hope will eventuate into a…' again he hunted awkwardly for the right words '…a live child.'

Giorgio saw the flicker of pain pass over her features. She was measuring herself in terms of whether she could deliver the goods. He wished then that he had thought of a better way to put it.

'I need to go to bed,' she said, as if that was the end of the discussion—for her. Her chin had gone up defensively, her slim shoulders were aligned tightly and there was a fiery light in her grey eyes that warned him not to push any further.

He reached down to anchor Gonzo's collar. 'I will

take this boy out for a block or two while you settle into bed. If you need me during the night, just call me.'

She gave him a very determined look. 'I don't need you, Giorgio,' she said crisply. 'I can do this alone if I have to.'

In spite of the dog's leaping excitement at the prospect of a late night walk, Giorgio still fixed his gaze on Maya's with intractability. Hearing her say she didn't need him any more triggered something deep and primal in his blood. He would not let her leave him for a second time without a fight, baby or no baby. 'You have said this is my child, Maya,' he said. 'I am not going to walk away from my own flesh and blood. I have changed my mind. Our marriage will continue indefinitely.'

CHAPTER SIX

OR UNTIL I lose this child, just like I lost all the others, Maya thought as Giorgio strode out of the flat with the dog at his side. She couldn't see him sticking out the long years of a fruitless marriage, not unless something other than duty and obligation bound him to it.

Something like love.

She chided herself for regressing into that fairyland of hope. She had long ago given up on him feeling anything for her. Why torture herself any more when it was even more unlikely he would ever change?

She left the small *salone* and took the opportunity while Giorgio was out to prepare for bed. She quickly removed her make-up and did her usual skincare routine. She looked at the expensive lotions and potions a little ruefully. She had been tempted to toss them out with all the other things she had been entitled to as a Sabbatini wife over the years, but she hated waste, or that was the reasoning she had used when she had packed her things the day she had left.

She didn't like thinking of that awful day. She had been cowardly about it by leaving when Giorgio was in Switzerland with his team of accountants at a huge financial conference in Zurich. She hadn't thought she would have the strength to go through with it with him there in person, even though over those last few months things had become rather tense and difficult between them. They had argued a lot, bickering over the silliest things just like a live-in couple or flatmates who were thoroughly sick of each other's irritating little habits.

Maya had found it so distressing to think he was starting to hate her. She often saw him looking at her with a brooding sort of expression, as if he wasn't quite sure what to do with her.

They hadn't made love in weeks…well, it had been more like three months. The hormone injections Maya had been given as part of the IVF plan had made her moody and irritable. And then Giorgio had had to provide a sample of sperm, which she knew he found undignified, even though the doctors and staff were totally professional about it.

Sex was a chore, a duty and it had killed any feeling he might have had for her once. Not that he had ever said he loved her. It wasn't part of their relationship. She had known that and married him anyway, hoping he would gradually develop feelings for her. But Giorgio wasn't a feeling type of man. She couldn't imagine him allowing himself to be vulnerable. He held everyone at a distance.

Maya had enough friends in her life to know not all relationships worked out. Even the most secure and settled couples could be torn apart by what life dished up. She had always prided herself that she would never give up on her man. She would be the loyal, loving wife, doing everything she could to make their relationship keep its zing and passion. But in the end she had failed. She had failed because it was not just about her role in the marriage, but Giorgio's too. He had slowly but surely drifted away from her. She had felt it subtly at first and she had been gracious about it, putting it down to the tragic loss of his father and how he had so much extra responsibility as a result.

Those three weeks with Giancarlo lying in a semi-conscious state had been one of the most heartbreaking things to witness. It had been cruel to see such a strong and fit man become so weak.

Maya had tried to support her mother-in-law as best she could during that horrific and tragic time, but Giovanna had pointedly clung to her sons and Maya had felt increasingly shut out. How could a new daughter-in-law offer comfort to that depth of grief? In the end she had stayed in the background, doing what she could when she could, hoping she wasn't inadvertently making things worse.

Maya's failure to maintain a pregnancy past six weeks had at one point the following year prompted Giovanna to mention how she had delivered three healthy sons and a daughter at regular intervals, the subtext being: what the hell was wrong with Maya for not being able to do the same? Maya had put it down to her mother-in-law's ongoing grief. Giovanna rarely left the family villa and the doctor had even prescribed some antidepressant medication to see if that would help.

No one in the Sabbatini family, apart from Salvatore,

had ever spoken about the death of baby Chiara all those years ago.

Maya had learned from Salvatore how Giorgio had been the one to find his sister lying cold and lifeless in her crib. He had been only six years old.

Not much more than a baby himself, certainly far too young to cope with such a loss.

When she had tried to talk to Giorgio about it after that distressing episode with his mother, as usual, he'd refused to discuss it, other than this time to say it belonged in the past and his mother was still grieving and Maya should have more sensitivity and patience.

Maya had been stung by his blocking attitude to more intimate communication. She saw it as a sign of what was essentially wrong with their relationship. He did not confide in her. He had never confided in her. He kept things to himself; he never showed any sign of vulnerability.

Not even when he came home from Switzerland to find her note propped up on the desk in his study had he reacted as she had secretly hoped he would. He had tracked her down within a day or two and informed her he would get the paperwork regarding the separation of assets in order. He'd spoken coldly and impersonally, as if he was discussing a legal issue with a business opponent. He'd shown no anger, no emotion at all, in fact. He had left within five minutes, barely even stopping long enough to pat Gonzo.

Maya had realised then how hopeless it all was; she had been right from the beginning. They were too different, their worlds too disparate. Just like Gonzo, she was a penniless, abandoned orphan with indiscriminate breeding. Giorgio belonged to a large extended blue-blooded family where money and wealth and privilege were never questioned.

The door opened downstairs and Maya quickly slipped into her bed, pulling the covers up to her chin. She snapped off the lamp, even though she would have loved to continue reading the book she had by the bedside. She found it almost impossible to sleep without reading for a few minutes. She closed her eyes, barely able to breathe, waiting to hear those firm foot treads on the stairs.

But there was nothing.

She didn't know whether to feel angry or grateful. But then she started to think of Giorgio trying to get comfortable on that wretched little sofa. She could picture him crunched up like a banana folded in half; his back was probably aching by now, his long legs having gone numb from hanging over the end of the sofa arms.

She turned over and faced the wall, her eyes opening to see the silvery eye of the moon staring back at her. She lay like that for endless minutes, listening for any sound of movement downstairs.

After a while there were footsteps on the stairs but they weren't Giorgio's. There was a distinctive scratching at the door and a little doggy please-let-me-in whine.

Maya rolled on her back and groaned. She had been trying to train Gonzo to sleep on his own cushion in the laundry, but he had apparently conveniently forgotten all about his humble beginnings and now, like all the other Sabbatinis, she knew, expected to sleep on one thousand threads of Egyptian cotton every night.

She threw off the covers and padded over to the door and opened it. 'No, Gonzo,' she said sternly. 'You have to sleep downstairs.' She pointed her finger in that direction. 'Go back down. *Now.*'

More footsteps sounded on the stairs and Maya's finger went limp, along with her legs, as Giorgio appeared in nothing but his tight-fitting underwear. Her eyes feasted on him like a starved animal presented with an all-you-can-eat banquet. Tightly ridged muscle carved the contours of his abdomen, his chest was sprinkled with masculine hair, the hair that used to tickle the sensitive skin of her breasts. It narrowed down over his stomach to disappear in a tantalising trail beneath the waistband of his underwear. Strictly speaking, he wasn't fully aroused but he wasn't far off it. The bulge of his manhood was stirring even as she could feel her body responding.

How she finally dragged her eyes back up to his was nothing short of a miracle. 'I can handle this,' she said in her best teacher-like voice. 'It's not the first time he's pulled this kind of stunt on me.'

Giorgio leaned one of his broad shoulders against the door jamb, which meant Maya had to move backwards and of course Gonzo, seizing the opportunity, rapidly squeezed past and leapt up on the bed, circling a couple of times before dropping and closing his eyes with a blissful sigh.

'Now look what you've done,' Maya said hotly. 'I've

been working on him for weeks and you've undone it just like that.' She snapped her fingers for effect.

Giorgio captured her hand in mid-air and brought it to his mouth, his lips playing with her fingers in a nibble-like caress, his dark glinting eyes tethering hers. 'It seems every male you know wants to share your bed, *cara*,' he said. 'I don't blame Gonzo. The sofa is singularly the most uncomfortable piece of furniture I have ever laid eyes on, let alone my body.'

Maya wrenched her hand away. 'Gonzo is supposed to be sleeping on his dog bed in the laundry which, I might tell you, I spent a lot of money on.'

He lifted one shoulder as if in full agreement with the hound. 'Your bed looks much more inviting.'

She folded her arms and did her best to stare him down. 'If you think I am going to share it with both of you then you can think again.'

He closed the door with his foot, the clicking of the latch sounding like a pistol firing in the silence

'Wh…what are you doing?' Maya asked, backing away.

His slow-moving sexy eyes ran over her satin nightgown, relishing the way the fabric clung to her breasts in all the right places. She felt the heat of her skin go up several degrees and her heart rate escalated, making her speech breathless and jerky. 'S…stop it, Giorgio. Stop it right this instant. You know sleeping together right now is out of the question. It's too dangerous.'

He cupped the back of her head with one large controlling hand, his body moving just that little bit closer, close enough for her to feel the effect she was having on him. 'Who said anything about sleeping?' he said. 'Besides, we can do other things to relieve this sexual tension.'

Maya knew exactly what sort of thing he was suggesting and it made her blood sing and thrum through her veins. Pleasuring each other without penetrative sex had been something they had done in the past, in the early exciting days of their marriage when nothing had been off limits. She had not realised her body could scale the heights of pleasure it had without his body doing all the work. He had introduced her to sensual delights that had shocked her at the time, but now they were like a delicious memory she wanted to revisit.

But wait...

How dared he stir her senses up like that? She was supposed to be demonstrating how immune she was to him, even if she wasn't. It would give him too much power to know she would be his again at the sexy stroke of his tongue or one of his fingers, that he could make her convulse uncontrollably with just a few clever caresses that would leave her body tingling for hours afterwards.

'Forget it, Giorgio,' she said, affecting a bored disinterested tone. 'I'm tired. I have no interest in your bedroom games.'

He captured her hands, pulling her up against him, rubbing his aroused length against her quivering belly. 'Go on, *tesore mio*,' he said in a smouldering spine-loosening tone, 'just like you used to do in the past.'

Maya's heart fluttered like a deck of rapidly shuffled cards. She was so tempted, so very dangerously tempted.

She could almost taste his salty muskiness, she could almost feel the satin-covered steely length of him filling her mouth, and she could almost feel the shuddering quake of his body as he finally tipped over the edge...

He moved his body against her again. He was powerfully erect. She had felt that hardened length sliding back and forth inside her so many delicious times in the past, the way it caught on the most sensitive part of her if she tilted her hips just that little bit higher, how he could smash her into a million pieces of ecstasy with a soft but sure flickering caress of his fingers against her swollen need.

All she had to do was drop to her knees in front of him, peel back his underwear and swirl her tongue over him, once, twice, waiting for him to suck in his breath.

But she wasn't going to do it.

Not now.

Not like this.

Not because he had an itch he wanted scratching. That was an itch any other woman could scratch. And plenty of other women had probably done so in the time they had been apart.

Maya steeled her resolve, which took some effort considering she had none in reserve. She was running on almost empty but it was enough to put some distance between them. 'You and Gonzo can have the bed,' she said, scooping up her wrap off the end of the bedpost. 'I will take the sofa.'

'You don't have to do that, Maya,' Giorgio said, pushing a hand through the lock of his hair that kept insisting on falling over his forehead. 'The paparazzi will have given up by now. I will go back to the hotel for the rest of the night. I will see you in the morning. Have your essential things packed. I will organise for the rest to be transported over later.'

Maya watched in frozen silence as he left the bedroom. She counted each and every one of his footsteps as he went down the stairs.

After a few minutes she heard a car arrive—she assumed it was a Sabbatini staff member summoned to pick him up—and then the sound of it pulling away from the kerb and disappearing into the night.

She turned and looked at Gonzo, who was sound asleep and snoring on her bed. She gave her head a little shake and slipped in beside him, or at least as far as his solid presence would allow. It was like trying to sleep on a corkboard, she thought as the minutes slowly ticked by. She was never going to be able to sleep, she was sure of it. But, somehow, the sound of the dog's rhythmic snuffles and snores and her own emotional and physical exhaustion took over. She rolled over, curling her legs into a comma shape to allow for Gonzo, and finally went to sleep...

CHAPTER SEVEN

THE doorbell pealed just as Maya had her head hanging over the basin in the bathroom. The nausea had caught her off guard. She had never felt anything like it before. It was like being on the worst sea voyage of her life. The world of her small rented flat was not stable; it was rocking all over the place. And it wasn't just the flat, it was the smell of things that assaulted her senses and sent them into revolt. She had opened a can of food for Gonzo at his insistence and then had to bolt upstairs to deal with the consequences. Her oesophagus felt raw, as if scraped by razorblades.

The doorbell rang again, this time with Gonzo's voluble accompaniment.

Maya groaned and wiped her whitewash-coloured face on the hand towel. Her eyes were like water drip holes in snow, hollow and shadowed with exhaustion.

She clung to the banister on the way down with a deathly grip, sure she was going to drop into a faint. But somehow she managed to get to the front door and opened it, bleary-eyed and sick as she was.

'*Dio!* What the hell?' Giorgio instantly sprang into action. He took her by the upper arms, holding her steady, sending a curt command to Gonzo to back off. 'Are you sick, Maya?' he asked, his frown so tense and serious it made his head ache.

'I've got the most awful nausea,' she said weakly. 'I've been sick for the last hour. Gonzo's food set me off...'

'Right, that settles it,' he said. 'I will send someone over to pack up your things. You need to rest. I will feed Gonzo in the future. You need to concentrate on looking after this baby. The first thing that needs to happen is a doctor's appointment. Right now, as soon as I can arrange it.'

She pushed back her damp blond hair from her pale forehead. 'I don't want to be told how likely it is I'm going to lose this baby,' she said, her chin wobbling slightly. 'I don't have a great track record.'

Giorgio felt a hand clutch at his insides. 'You are not going to lose this baby, not if I can help it.'

She looked up at him with a pained expression. 'You can't control everything, Giorgio; surely you realise that by now?'

He refused to consider the possibility of failure. He set his jaw, pushing it forward indomitably. 'We have got this far, Maya,' he said. 'I know it is still early days but you are extremely nauseous. I think I read somewhere that it is a good sign of strong hormonal activity when a woman is so nauseous in the early days of pregnancy. We have to cling to that. To hope that this one will be the success we have hoped for all this time.'

She turned away from him, her shoulders slumped forward as if already preparing for defeat. 'I'm so frightened to hope,' she said in a whisper-soft voice. 'I feel like a gift has been handed to me but it's not quite in my hands. I can't help feeling it will be snatched away at the last minute if I get my hopes up.'

'You can't think like that, Maya,' he insisted. 'You have to remain positive.'

She turned and faced him. 'There are no guarantees, though, are there?' she asked. 'I know you don't like talking about it but you lost your sister when she was three months old. She was a living, breathing, interactive baby. This baby is a tiny embryo, not even independent of my body. What hope is there that we won't lose him or her in the future, just like your little sister?'

A shutter came down over his face, just like a heavy curtain over a stage. Maya knew she had overstepped the mark. She had mentioned the unmentionable. But she longed to be reassured, she longed for the confidence she lacked—that this pregnancy would be the glue that would stick their marriage back into place.

'This is an entirely different situation,' he said in a flat emotionless tone. 'We have been down this path before. It is tricky and uncertain but there are things we can cling to in hope this time around. This is a natural conception, one that occurred a long time after your previous miscarriages. This is a totally different ballgame. We did this all by ourselves: no hormone injections, no temperature charts—we just got down and did what had to be done and now we are expecting a baby. We have to go with this; we have to take it as it comes.'

She pressed her lips together, making them as white as her face. 'And if we fail?'

He gave her a look of steely determination. 'We are not going to fail, Maya, not this time.'

Maya longed for his confidence, if indeed what he was exhibiting was confidence. She had a feeling he was as worried as she was, but he was not letting on. 'Giorgio...' she began uncertainly. 'What did you feel when I lost the other babies?'

He drew in a breath and let it out in a slow uneven stream. 'I was devastated for you and for me. I know I didn't show it, but it's what I've always done in a crisis.' He paused. 'I had to be strong so you could lean on me. I didn't realise until now how wrong that approach probably was.'

'I wish I had known that's how you felt...'

'Would it have made a difference?' he asked.

Maya let her shoulders drop. 'I don't know...'

He touched her cheek with two fingers. 'I didn't want to burden you with my own sense of failure. I felt you had enough to deal with. But now I see I should have shared more with you about how it felt for me so you understood that I knew at least some of what you were feeling.'

It explained a lot, Maya thought, and yet she was still worried about his motives for keeping their marriage on track. If she failed to deliver a live child, would he still insist on their marriage continuing? And, even if she did give birth to the heir he so dearly wanted, wouldn't she then have to live with the knowledge she was the mother of a Sabbatini heir and not the love of his life, as she so dearly longed to be?

'Have you told your grandfather about this pregnancy?' she asked.

He dropped his hand from her face. 'No, but I think
we should tell him as soon as possible. It would boost his
spirits no end to know he might be a great-grandfather
again in a few months. I only wish he could live that
long to see it eventuate.'

Maya felt the pain of his statement. It was as raw for
her as it was for him. She still could not quite believe
the vibrant, cheeky patriarch of the family was facing
imminent death. She could not imagine life without
him. It would be doubly hard for Giorgio. He would be
expected to carry the family through the crisis while
holding the Sabbatini empire in place.

'I wish he could live that long too,' she said softly.

'We'll tell him as soon as we get back from the
doctor,' he said. 'Now, do you need a hand getting
ready? I have my car outside. We can go straight to the
surgery.'

Maya pushed a hand through her limp hair. 'I need
to have a shower…'

'Have a quick one while I call the doctor,' he said,
pulling out his mobile. 'I'll get one of my staff to come
and collect Gonzo and your things and take them to the
villa.'

It was all happening so fast that Maya could barely
keep up. Giorgio was in organising mode and he was
letting nothing stand in his way. After fighting to be
independent for so long, she perversely began to feel
the relief of having someone take control. It made her

feel protected and sheltered from having to worry about things all on her own.

The shower did much to restore her equilibrium. The worst of the nausea had abated and when she came downstairs dressed in jeans and a rollneck cashmere sweater with a trench coat draped around her shoulders in case it was still cold outside, Giorgio was already waiting for her.

He gave her a rare smile, such a small movement of his lips but it still managed to contract her heart. 'You look a lot better. Not feeling so sick now?' he asked.

She shook her head. 'No, I'm fine now.'

He held the door open for her, commanding Gonzo to sit on his cushion in the laundry instead of bolting out of the door, as clearly had been the dog's plan.

'He is getting out of control,' Giorgio said as he led Maya to his car, parked illegally in front of her flat. 'You've clearly been too soft with him.'

She sent him a resentful little glare as he activated the remote control device to unlock the car. 'He's been upset by the change in living arrangements,' she said. 'Now I can understand how children misbehave for one or both of their parents when there is a divorce. It's very unsettling having to shift between two residences all the time.'

He held open the passenger door for her. 'I wasn't the one who instigated the divorce,' he reminded her with a speaking look.

'No, but you would have got around to it sooner or later,' she said.

He didn't answer other than to close the door and

stride around to the driver's side, his expression dark and brooding.

Maya pulled down the seat belt with an angry movement of her hand. She waited until he was sitting in the driver's seat beside her before she said, 'I'm doing my best, Giorgio. I haven't deliberately spoilt Gonzo. He misses you, that's all. I didn't realise how much until we had separated.'

He looked across at her for a pulsing moment, his eyes inscrutable and impossibly dark. 'Well, he will not have to worry about that now.'

Maya tied her fingers into a knot in her lap. 'We haven't really discussed this properly,' she said. 'You said our marriage is to continue indefinitely, but that is not just up to you. I have some say in it, surely?'

He started the car with a rocket-fuel roar, putting it into gear with a savage movement of his hand. 'You, for once, Maya, will do as you are told. I am tired of being painted as the bad guy in all of this. I have done the best I could do under the circumstances. I know I am not the best husband in the world, but neither am I the worst. We've had some bad luck. Lots of people do, even worse things than we've experienced. We should both be mature enough to deal with it and move on.'

Maya clenched her teeth to stop herself from flinging an invective his way. He always made it seem as if she was the one who was being childish and petty, giving up in a pout when she should have pressed on. The nine-year age gap between them didn't help. It gave him an edge in experience that she couldn't see how she could ever make up.

'But we have nothing in common,' she said. 'I don't see how we can make our marriage work when it's already failed once.'

'We have more in common than you realise,' he said. 'We both love dogs, for instance.'

She rolled her eyes at him. 'Lots of people love dogs. It doesn't mean they would make a great life partner.'

'It's a start, Maya,' he said. 'And we're sexually compatible. You can't deny that now, can you?'

Maya turned her gaze away as she felt the stirring of her body. She quickly crossed her legs, hoping to suppress it but, if anything, it made her more aware of her need of him.

One of his hands reached across and squeezed hers. 'Just in case there are paparazzi around, put on a happy face, Maya,' he said. 'It's really important my grandfather believes this to be a genuine reconciliation.'

Maya glanced at him as he took his hand away to change gear. 'You don't feel uncomfortable about lying to him?' she asked. 'You've always been close to him. Don't you think he will see through this charade for what it is?'

He gave a little up and down movement of his shoulders. 'I don't see that I am lying to him at all,' he said. 'This is what I want right now. A divorce is out of the question.'

She frowned as she studied his expression as he focused on the traffic ahead. 'You didn't exactly beg me to return to you when I instigated proceedings, though, did you?'

He sent her a quick inscrutable glance before turning

back to the road in front. 'I knew I was making you unhappy. There seemed no point in continuing to make you miserable just to keep up appearances. Anyway, you should know me well enough by now to know it's not in my nature to beg.'

There was that damn Sabbatini pride raising its head again, Maya thought. 'So the only way to get me back was to blackmail me emotionally,' she said. 'You knew I wouldn't say no to Salvatore, so you used his illness to your advantage.'

'You make it sound as if I have engineered his illness for my own gain,' Giorgio said. 'I would give anything to keep my grandfather alive for another ten years but that is not what fate has decided.'

'All the same, this situation really works to your advantage, doesn't it?' she said. 'You get to stall a very expensive divorce for a few more weeks, if not months.'

He looked at her as if she was a small, disobedient child he was reprimanding. 'It could be years, Maya. You need to get your head around that. Sabbatinis do not take divorce lightly.'

She sent him a hot little glare. 'Do you think I care a fig for your black credit card lifestyle? Money can buy you a lot of things, but it can't buy the most valuable thing in life.'

'You seemed to enjoy what came your way,' he said with a tightening of his mouth. 'I didn't hear any complaints about the holidays and jewellery and designer wardrobe.'

'You might not have noticed but I left a lot of what you gave me behind,' she said, 'including my rings.'

'I have them in safe keeping for you,' he said. 'They are in the safe at my villa. I want you to wear them from now on.'

Maya wanted to tell him exactly where he could put his rings, but she reminded herself that this was about making Salvatore happy in the remaining weeks of his life. It wasn't the time to be scoring points with Giorgio; it was the time for a truce, so he could prepare himself and the rest of his family for the sad end of his grand-father's long and productive life.

The doctor's waiting room was almost full but Maya and Giorgio were led straight through to the doctor who had treated Maya in the past.

Dr Rossini was surprisingly optimistic about the pregnancy progressing to full-term this time around. 'You are in excellent health, Signora Sabbatini,' he said. 'You are perhaps a little underweight but that will soon change with a better diet and more rest. I will do a full blood test screen. The home test you used is very reliable so if you like we can do an intravaginal ultrasound in my examination room next door to make sure everything is as it should be, given your history.'

'Do you want me to wait outside?' Giorgio asked Maya.

Although the procedure was more invasively intimate than an abdominal ultrasound, Maya shook her head. She did not have it in herself to deny Giorgio the first glimpse of their baby and she felt in very great need of his support. 'No, please stay.'

'Come through.' Dr Rossini directed them to the room

next door. He left them for a few minutes while Maya got on the examination table, undressing her lower body and covering herself with a blanket in preparation.

She sent Giorgio a worried glance but he gave her a reassuring smile. 'Try not to worry, *cara*,' he said. 'The doctor seems pretty confident you and the baby will be fine.'

Dr Rossini came in and gloved up, talking them through the procedure, as well as pointing out the tiny embryo, which was just four centimetres long. 'You can see a tiny heartbeat just there.' He showed them on the screen. 'The C-shaped curvature is developing and those little buds there in the next few weeks will become legs and arms. Your baby looks a healthy little one so far. Congratulations.'

Maya could do nothing about the tears that rolled from her eyes as the doctor put away his equipment. Giorgio silently handed her a crisp white handkerchief, his own eyes suspiciously moist. It was too soon to hope, she kept saying to herself. She'd had early ultrasounds before and still lost the baby, but she couldn't help thinking that something felt different about this one. Was she imagining the tiny shape on the screen looked more robust than the previous ones in the first two years of their marriage?

The drive to Giorgio's villa was conducted in a silence that was tense but not antagonistic. Maya wondered what he was thinking, whether he was nervous, excited or worried or all three. She glanced at him now and again, searching for some clue to what he was feeling, but he was concentrating on the traffic, a small frown bringing his brows together over his eyes.

They arrived at the villa and Maya had to blink a couple of times as he had changed the colour scheme of the outside. Extensive work had been done in the gardens too, and he had installed an infinity pool on one of the terraces that in spring and summer enjoyed full sun.

Inside was just as transformed. Fresh curtains and festooned pelmets hung at the windows, the marbled floors were polished and the grand staircase was recarpeted in an ankle-deep runner that wound its way up like a river. The smell of fresh paint was prominent in the air but it gave the villa a new, hopeful and revitalised atmosphere.

'What do you think?' Giorgio asked as he showed her through the downstairs rooms.

'It's…it's amazing,' Maya said, turning in a full circle to take all of the changes in. 'The colours are lovely. I couldn't have done better myself. Did you employ an interior designer?'

He gave her a wry look. 'A whole team of them. I wanted to freshen up the place. I felt it needed a change.'

Maya wondered again if that had had more to do with removing every trace of her presence, but she had cause to rethink that opinion when he showed her the upstairs bedroom they used to share. He had knocked down a wall to create more space and installed a walk-in wardrobe along with a brand-new en suite bathroom that was twice the size of the one they had had before.

It had a deep bowl-like bathtub set in the middle of the room and a double headed glass shower unit in one corner. Twin basins with gilt-edged mirrors above and cupboards beneath completed the transformation.

The walk-in wardrobe off the bedroom suite was almost as big as the kitchen at her rented flat. But what was more surprising was that all of the clothes and other accessories she had left behind were hanging in neat rows or folded in the drawer section as if she had never left.

She turned from inspecting it all to look up at him. 'Why didn't you toss out all of the stuff I left behind or send it to a charity or something?'

He gave a movement of his lips that was the equivalent of a dismissive shrug, but behind his eyes a glint of triumph gleamed as he handed her the engagement and wedding rings she had left next to her departure note all those months ago. 'It's called hedging your bets,' he said. 'I took a gamble. It paid off. I had a feeling you might change your mind once you realised what you were throwing away.'

CHAPTER EIGHT

IF IT hadn't been for his grandfather's illness and the precarious state of his health, Maya would have walked out right then and there, just to prove him wrong.

'Your confidence is misplaced, Giorgio,' she said with a tart edge to her voice as she shoved the rings on her finger. 'You know I am only here now because of your grandfather and the baby, both of whom could be gone within a matter of weeks.'

His brows snapped together. 'Stop talking like that. It's almost as if you want to lose this child. You heard what the doctor said. There is no reason to be so negative. You are in good health and the baby looks healthy for its age and stage.'

She glared back at him with her arms crossed over her middle. 'Don't tell me what I can and can't say or what I can and can't feel.'

Giorgio raked a hand through his hair but it did little to restore any order to it. If anything, it made Maya want to run her hands through it as she used to do. The temptation to do so was suddenly almost too much to bear. She needed his touch for reassurance. Coming back to the villa, as changed as it was, still affected her deeply. Just a few metres down the hall was the nursery she had so excitedly prepared all those years ago. Had he stripped it until it too was unrecognisable?

She was too frightened to ask.

'Maya.' He came over to where she was standing so stiffly and placed his hands gently on the top of her shoulders. 'Forgive me,' he said gruffly. 'I am forgetting you are in the midst of a hormonal turmoil, let alone worrying about what's happened in the past. I am worried too. I am desperately worried I won't do or say the right thing, just like I did before. I am still learning how to do this. It's all new to me. This time I want things to be perfect for you and the baby. Believe me, *cara*, I don't want to upset you now. I don't want to fight with you. I want to look after you.'

She took a steadying breath as she looked into his dark gaze. 'What did you do with the nursery?' she asked.

His hands tightened for a nanosecond on her shoulders before he removed them to hang by his sides. His expression threatened to lock down as usual, but then she saw a tiny fist punching beneath the skin at the edge of his mouth, as if trying to push its way through. A war was going on within him; the effort to override his instinctive response was clearly taking a huge toll. 'I had it redecorated,' he said. 'It's a spare bedroom now.'

She disguised a quick apprehensive swallow. 'Can I see it?'

He stepped aside to hold the door open for her. 'Of course.'

Maya walked down the hall, unable to shake off the

feeling of walking back through time. She had been so excited during that first pregnancy. She had shopped and shopped, filling the villa with baby things, from teddy bears to teething rings. She had bought clothing: tiny all in one suits, booties and nappies and bibs. She had even taught herself to knit and in the evenings she would make some very odd-shaped booties until she finally got the hang of it. She had insisted on choosing and then papering the walls of the nursery herself. She had made it a project, to make the most beautiful nursery with everything ready and waiting for their precious baby.

And then she had miscarried.

The nursery had seemed to mock her with its array of baby goods each time she walked past it. After a few months she conceived again and, buoyed up with renewed hope and the optimism of youth, she had started nesting again.

By the fourth miscarriage she had learned her lesson and learned it well. She had closed the door and had never opened it since.

Opening it now was like opening a wound that had not quite healed. The sound of the handle turning felt like someone picking at the scab, pain sliced through her—the pain of loss, of disappointment, of failure and hopelessness.

The room was decorated in a duck egg blue and cream. It looked nothing like a nursery. It was just a spare bedroom, a rather beautifully appointed one with Parisian-style furniture.

'It's very...nice,' she said as the silence swirled around her. She turned and faced him, pasting a smile on her face that made her muscles ache. 'You've done a good job. No one would ever think it was once a...' she forced the word out '...a nursery.'

Giorgio reached for her and she stumbled forwards into his arms, burying her face against his chest. He cupped his hand at the back of her head, holding her to him, knowing there were no words that could take away the hurt of the past. He stood with her in the circle of his arms for several minutes, breathing in her scent, enjoying the neat fit of her body against his.

After a while she eased out of his embrace and swiped at her damp eyes with the backs of her hands. 'Sorry,' she said with a self-conscious grimace. 'It must be the hormones. I feel uncharacteristically weepy.'

He brushed the hair back from her cheek with a gentle finger. 'It's understandable,' he said. He paused for a moment before he continued, 'It was so difficult when I gave the go-ahead to redecorate that room. I felt like I was giving up on everything we had both wanted. It intensified my sense of failure.'

She tried to smile but it came out lopsided, making her seem much younger than her years. 'I hope Gonzo doesn't put his dirty paws on all the new furniture,' she said.

'I am sure he will behave himself once he is back in his old routine,' Giorgio said. 'He should be here soon, along with your things. By the way, I have dealt with the lease on your flat. I paid a couple of months extra to keep the landlord sweet about terminating the lease ahead of time. I've also sorted out the London premises you had lined up.'

'Thank you,' she said, shifting her gaze out of the range of his. 'It seems you've thought of everything.'

'It's my job to see to details, Maya,' he said. 'Now, if you are not too tired, I think it would be good to call on my grandfather and tell him our news. Do you feel up to it?'

'Of course,' she said with another not-quite-all-the-way smile.

Salvatore had not long informed the rest of the close members of his family about his prognosis.

Giovanna was weeping but seemed to collect herself once Giorgio and Maya came in. She kissed her eldest son and then turned to Maya, her greeting a little warmer than the night before. 'I am so glad you are back with my son,' she said. 'This is such a sad time but at least I can be assured now that you and Giorgio will not make things any worse by divorcing.'

Maya answered something non-committal.

Luca was looking shell-shocked but resigned and Nic was looking bored, leaning indolently against a bookcase as if he had better things to do and see, but Maya knew it was probably a mask covering what he was really feeling. More like Giorgio than he wanted to admit, Nic didn't like to show his emotions too freely.

Giorgio assembled everyone together once he made sure his grandfather was comfortable. 'Maya and I have some news,' he said. 'It's very early days and we don't want any of you to rush off and buy gifts or anything, but we have just had Maya's pregnancy confirmed.'

Giovanna's mouth fell open. '*So soon?* But you've

only spent one night back together. How can you know if it's—'

'*Mamma...*' Giorgio began sternly.

'Was it the night of my wedding?' Luca asked with a twinkle in his eye. 'I know you were putting on a reasonable show of civility for Bronte and I on our special day, but I saw you looking daggers at each other every now and again when you thought no one was looking. The air was crackling like an electric current. Everyone was commenting on it.'

Maya felt herself blushing to the roots of her hair. 'I'm sorry if it was that obvious... I hope we didn't offend you and Bronte.'

'Not at all,' Luca said, still grinning. 'If this is the outcome, I couldn't be more thrilled.'

Giorgio reached for Maya's hand and enfolded it within his. 'We are thrilled as well,' he said. 'This baby is very special to us. We have been given a second chance and this time we are not going to waste it. Whatever happens, we are staying together.'

Giovanna, to her credit, came over and hugged Maya, expressing her delight in a mixture of Italian and English. It reminded Maya of the early days, when she had felt a tentative closeness to her mother-in-law, before the death of Giancarlo and the loss of her babies had ruined everything.

Luca swept Maya up into a brotherly hug, congratulating them both, before rushing off so he could tell Bronte, who had stayed back at their villa with Ella, who was sleeping.

Nic sauntered over with a mocking smile on his face,

his green-flecked hazel eyes flicking to Maya's belly and then to his brother's face. 'Nice job,' he said. 'I knew you had it in you. Now all you have to do is keep her with you…oh, and make sure it's actually yours, as *Mamma* hinted at earlier.'

Giorgio swore at his youngest brother, his fist clenching at his side as if he was tempted to use it. 'There is no doubt in my mind this is my child,' he said through gritted teeth.

'Maya…' Salvatore's voice broke up the tense scene.

She went over to where he was sitting and took both of his outstretched hands in hers. 'Are you happy for us, Salvatore?' she asked, trying to keep her voice from cracking with emotion.

His eyes were glistening with moisture and his grip on her hands was almost crushing in his joy. 'I can now die a happy man,' he said. 'I know this baby will survive. I have prayed for this. God gives one life and takes one away. It is the order of things, *si*?'

Maya wasn't too happy with God over taking away her previous pregnancies, but she wasn't going to do or say anything to take away from the old man's faith. 'I'm very happy too,' she said. 'I still can't quite believe it. It seems like a miracle.'

'It *is* a miracle,' Salvatore said. 'And now all I have to do is see my youngest grandson settled and my life's work will be complete.'

Nic muttered something under his breath and Giorgio shot him a reproachful look.

Having grown up without siblings, it had taken Maya

a while to get used to the way the Sabbatini sons related
to each other. There was certainly a pecking order and
Luca, though strong, did not often contest the top position. Nic, on the other hand, was too like Giorgio to want
to bow down to his command just because he was the
younger by four years. They often had power struggles
that went on for days, sometimes weeks. Giorgio thought
Nic needed to grow up and take more responsibility for
his life. Nic thought Giorgio was a control freak who
needed to get a life instead of trying to control everyone
else's.

'I want champagne,' Salvatore announced. 'Not for
you, Maya, *mio piccolo*, but we must toast this baby.
Giorgio, call one of the staff to send some up.'

A few minutes later, with glasses clinking and happy
laughter ringing, it didn't seem possible that the family
had been gathered together to be told of Salvatore's illness. It was like another party. Salvatore was in his
element, enjoying the moment for what it was: the celebration of the continuation of the Sabbatini dynasty.

But, like all good parties, this one had to come to an
end. Salvatore started to look tired and pale and Giorgio
immediately swung into action. With the live-in nurse's
help, he escorted his grandfather upstairs to his bedroom
and made sure he was settled and comfortable before
he left.

'Giorgio,' Salvatore said from the bed just as Giorgio
was about to leave, 'I want you to do something for
me.'

'Anything, *Nonno*,' Giorgio said.

Salvatore took a breath that rattled inside his damaged

lungs. 'I want you to send for Jade Sommerville, my god-daughter in London. I want to say goodbye to her before it's too late.'

Giorgio frowned. The last he had heard, the wild-child daughter of his grandfather's business associate Keith Sommerville had yet again disgraced the family name by having an affair with a married man. But Salvatore had always had a soft spot for the wilful Jade. Over the years he had always made excuses for her appalling behaviour, insisting she was damaged by the desertion of her sluttish mother at a young age. Giorgio was more of the opinion that Jade was exactly like her sleep-around mother and should be left to self-destruct, just as Harriet Sommerville had done some twenty-odd years ago. 'If that is what you wish,' he said. 'I will see if I can get her to agree to fly over for a few days.'

'Thank you…' Salvatore's breathing became even more laboured and the nurse bustled over to place an oxygen mask over his face to assist his breathing.

Giorgio moved forward to help but Salvatore waved him away, mumbling through his mask, 'Leave me now, Giorgio. I will be fine. Just make sure you contact Jade for me.'

'How is he?' Maya asked when Giorgio rejoined her back downstairs in the *salone*.

'Not good,' he said grimly. 'I don't think he's got as long as the doctors have said. Perhaps they were trying to give him hope, to help him remain positive.'

Maya felt a tight hand curl around her heart. 'If only he doesn't have to suffer…I couldn't bear that…'

He trailed his finger down the under curve of her cheek. 'He has morphine on demand,' he said. 'The nurse is with him twenty-four seven. It's all we can do at this stage.'

Maya didn't move away from Giorgio's closeness. She could feel his body heat and wanted to lean into him as she had done before. How wonderful it had been to feel the warm comfort of his arms around her, to pretend, even for a moment, he cared for her. 'You are a wonderful grandson, Giorgio,' she said. 'In fact you are wonderful to all of your family. I sometimes think they rely on you too much. They expect such a lot from you.' Her gaze dropped as she bit down into her bottom lip and added, 'Maybe I expected too much of you too.'

He lifted her chin with the end of his finger, locking his gaze with hers. 'I should have given you more,' he said. 'But maybe this time it will be different. It *feels* different, *cara*. I don't know about you, but it feels completely different this time around.'

Maya searched his expression for a moment. 'You mean about the baby?'

He leaned forward and pressed a barely touching kiss to her forehead. 'I mean about everything,' he said.

'Signor Sabbatini?' A staff member appeared at the door carrying a cordless phone. 'There is a phone call for you from a relative in Rome. They want an update on your grandfather's health.'

Maya had to suppress her disappointment at being interrupted at such a time. But, even so, there was no point in forcing Giorgio to reveal his feelings, if indeed he had any regarding her. It was all so muddied now with the prospect of a baby. Of course he would feel everything was different now. He was looking forward to having an heir, especially now, with his grandfather's life drawing to an imminent close.

It was as he had said: *everything* was different now.

They left a short time later after saying goodbye to Giorgio's mother, who had lived with Salvatore since Giancarlo had died.

Once they were back at Giorgio's villa a wave of tiredness swept over Maya. He noticed immediately and insisted she go upstairs and slip into bed.

Maya suddenly realised he meant *his* bed, the bed they had once shared as husband and wife. 'Where are you planning to sleep?' she asked, looking at him suspiciously.

'Where do you think I am going to sleep?' he said. 'In my bed, of course.'

'But we…we're not supposed to sleep together,' she faltered.

'The doctor didn't say we shouldn't,' he said. 'I specifically asked him while you were getting dressed in the ultrasound room. He just said to be careful, not to be too vigorous about it.'

Maya was incensed he had discussed it without her being there but, then again, she thought she might have found it excruciatingly embarrassing if he had. 'I didn't agree to resume a physical relationship with you as if nothing has changed,' she said. 'We've been separated for months. You can't expect me to jump back into bed with you as if nothing drove me out of it in the first place.'

'You left, not me,' he said in a clipped I-am-nearing-the-end-of-my-patience tone. 'And anyway, you jumped back into it pretty quickly once you had the chance. I barely touched you that night before you were tearing at me like a wild woman.'

Maya had never slapped anyone in her life. She abhorred violence of any sort, but somehow, without her even realising she was doing it until it was too late, her hand flew through the air and connected with the side of his jaw in a stinging slap that jerked his head sideways.

She watched in silent horror as a dark red angry patch appeared on the side of his face. She put both of her hands up to her mouth, covering her gasp of shock at what she had done.

The air tightened as if someone was pulling it from opposite ends of the room.

Anger, disgust and scorn burned in Giorgio's gaze as it held hers.

Fear, shame and remorse filled Maya's eyes with tears. 'I'm sorry…' She choked over the words. 'I don't know what came over me…I'm so sorry… Did I hurt you?'

He moved a step closer, taking her still stinging hand and placing it on the side of his face, holding it there like a cold press. His eyes continued to hold hers, but they had lost their glint of anger. His mouth lifted upwards in a wry version of a smile. 'You really are surging with hormones, aren't you, *tesore mio*?' he said. 'I have never known you to strike out like that, but then I think perhaps I deserved it, *si*?'

'No, it was wrong of me.' Maya removed her hand from his face and, stepping up on tiptoe, placed her lips there instead. Her lips clung like silk to sandpaper to the stubble on his jaw. Her breath stalled as she filled her nostrils with his male scent: the grace notes of lemon on a citrus stave.

Time froze in place, as if someone had blocked the second hand of the clock from ticking any further.

Maya felt her breath hitch in her throat as it got started again, her eyelids fluttering and then closing in silent surrender as Giorgio's mouth came down and covered hers.

CHAPTER NINE

THE thing that most took Maya by surprise was how tender Giorgio's kiss was. The night of his brother's wedding, the passion had flared like a struck match. They had both hungrily fed off each other's mouths like wild animals. It had been primal and sizzling and totally out of control.

This was different.

So exquisitely, breathtakingly different.

This was slow and sensual but no less sizzling. She felt the heat come up from her toes, melting her spine along the way, pooling in a lake of need at the very core of her being.

His tongue stroked ever so softly against the seam of her mouth and she opened to him, sighing with pleasure as he slid through to meet hers, curling around it like old lovers embracing after a long absence.

He tasted so familiar and yet so dangerously new: exciting and exotic, tantalisingly male and torturously tempting. Her tongue flirted with his, any thought of not following through with this long gone now. She wanted more of his kiss, more of his touch, more of what he had given her during that night just over six weeks ago, more of what she had secretly longed for ever since.

His mouth continued its tender assault on hers as his hands moved to the small of her back, pressing her into the hardened warmth of his body. She felt his erection, that delicious reminder of the power and potency that was hers for the asking. How could she say no to this? Her body was already screaming for the release it craved. She felt it in every pore of her skin, the tightening, tingling feeling of crawling need that overruled any common sense she possessed.

His hands moved again, this time to unbutton her shirt, button by button, each deliberately slow movement of his fingers ramping up her need. She felt the brush of his fingertips in the valley of her cleavage, her skin bursting into joy at that brief contact.

She pushed up against him, a silent plea for more. He gave it, lowering his mouth to her now uncovered breast, suckling on it hotly, teasing the tight nipple with his teeth until she gasped at the sensations rushing through her like a torrent. Her breasts seemed overly sensitive and she felt her inner core responding to each and every caress of his lips and tongue. It was unlike anything she had felt before.

'You feel bigger,' he said in a low sexy voice as he moved to her other breast.

'Hormones,' she managed to croak out as he took her other breast in his mouth and sent her off on another tingling journey of delight.

His mouth came back to hers and kissed her with renewed purpose. There was an edginess about his kiss, as if his passion for her was being stoked beyond his earlier control. Maya urged him on, not caring that she might regret her actions later. This was about now, about having her needs met and meeting his.

'*Dio*,' Giorgio said, tearing his mouth away and breathing hard. 'I don't think I can do this. I might not be able to control myself. I might hurt you or the baby.'

Disappointment was like a slap with an ice-cold wet towel. 'You said the doctor said it would be all right,' she said, tying her arms around his neck to stop him pulling away.

His chest rose and fell against hers. 'Maya, I want you so badly.'

She pulled his head back down to his. 'Then have me,' she whispered against his mouth.

He lifted her in his arms as if she weighed practically nothing and carried her upstairs to the master bedroom. He laid her on the bed, dispensing of his clothes, watching with furnace-hot eyes as she did the same with hers.

He came down beside her, placing one leg over her to balance his weight, careful not to crush her, his mouth covering hers again in a kiss which stoked the fire that was burning deep inside her.

She reached between their bodies to take him in her hand, to feel that glorious silky length of him, to feel the thunder of his blood against the curl of her fingers. She began to stroke him rhythmically, the up and down sweep of her hand inciting a growl of desire from the back of his throat. She saw him suck in his ridged abdomen and secretly delighted in the feminine power she had over him.

He pushed her hand away with a grunt and began to kiss his way down her body, starting at her breasts, travelling down her sternum, lingering over the tiny pucker of her belly button, before going to the cleanly waxed heart of her. He touched the soft naked skin, his eyes gleaming with pleasure. 'I noticed how sexy you looked when we were at the doctor's,' he said. 'I thought you might have stopped waxing after we separated.'

'I got used to it like this,' she said, wriggling so his fingers kept working their magic. 'It feels fresher.'

'It's so damn sexy,' he said, bringing his mouth down to taste her.

Maya lifted her back off the bed in response. She was so close to going over the edge, every nerve was twitching and dancing, poised to let go. But he made her wait. He strung out her pleasure, leading her to the edge again and again before pulling her back before she could freefall into oblivion. In the end she was almost weeping, begging him to let her come.

Finally he gave her what she wanted, but not quite how she wanted it. He used his mouth and tongue with clever little licks and flicks that sent her into a thousand pieces of pleasure, her whole body shook and rocked with it, making her shudder with the aftershocks.

'Now it's my turn,' he said, bringing her hand back down to his erection.

'But don't you want to…?' *How silly*, she thought, to be so coy about something they had done so many times in the past. 'Don't you want to come inside me?'

He kissed her neck, nuzzling there until she squirmed as her skin tingled in response. 'Of course I do but no rough sex until we get the all-clear,' he said. 'You know exactly what speed and pressure I like.'

Maya did as he said, her belly quivering in excitement as she watched him prepare to let go. Her hand tightened around him, the slippery movements making him tense all over before he spilled over her stomach with a guttural groan of release, such an intimate act, so raw, so intensely erotic.

She lay back, looking at him, wondering if he had any idea how much she loved him. He could so easily have insisted on full on sex, but he hadn't. He had done all he could to protect their tiny baby.

The baby he wanted more than anything.

The baby he wanted more than her.

It was a painful reminder of the tenuous position she was in. He was insisting their marriage would continue, regardless of whether or not they were successful in having a child, but what sort of marriage would that be? Would he have numerous affairs, as his father had done years ago until he had finally settled down? Would she be as forgiving as Giovanna had been? Maya wasn't so sure she could handle a philandering husband. Turning a blind eye required much more strength and confidence than she possessed.

Giorgio rose from the bed and reached for his trousers.

'Where are you going?' Maya asked.

'To get you a cool drink and something to eat,' he said, sliding up his zip. 'It's been ages since we left my grandfather's place. You need to keep your nourishment up.'

It was all about the baby, Maya thought as she turned her back to stare at the wall once he had left. *Please, my precious little baby, don't die on me*, she begged as she placed a gentle hand on her abdomen. *Please, please, please...*

When Giorgio came back with a drink and some food on a tray Maya was soundly asleep. She was curled up with one of her hands tucked under her cheek, the dark fan of her eyelashes such a contrast to her platinum blond hair.

He set the tray down carefully and sat on the edge of the bed, just watching her.

Sometimes he found it hard to unravel what he felt about his wife. He had never intended to fall in love with her or anyone. For most of his life he had worked hard to keep his emotions in check. He had shut off his feelings to protect himself, just as he had done when he had found his baby sister lying cold in her cot. The shattered emotions of his parents had terrified him as a child; he had imagined he or one of his brothers would be next to die unexpectedly, or even one of his parents. It had affected him far more deeply than he had ever let on, mostly for his parents' sake. They had needed him to be strong, to be there for his younger brothers, just as he'd had to be strong when his father was injured and subsequently died. There had not been time for his own grief to surface. He'd had to see to the business side of things: to arrange the massive funeral, to transfer all the important documents into his name and so on. He had switched to automatic. He had done it so often during his life that most of the time he wasn't even aware he was doing it any more.

Emotion frightened him. The vulnerability of loving too much terrified him. Loving someone too much left you open to unthinkable pain if they were taken away from you.

He saw it in Maya, the way she let her emotions control her until there *was* no control. She was at the mercy of her feelings, tossed about and worn out by them instead of facing things rationally.

But then that was Maya, the woman he had been attracted to from the first moment he had met her. Shy, virginal, not sure of herself, a little girl lost looking for a large family to envelop and protect her.

He reached out and brushed a strand of her hair back off her cheek. She let out a tiny sigh, her lips fluttering with the movement of air, just like a child's. He looked down at where her other hand was pressed, softly and protectively against her belly.

He felt his heart give a painful squeeze and he gently laid his hand over the top of hers and silently prayed for the child they had conceived, not in love and mutual desire, but in anger and bitterness.

Giorgio hoped to God it would not suffer for his sins.

Maya woke during the night and found Giorgio lying propped up on one elbow watching her in the light of the moon that shone in from one of the windows. There was a slight frown over his eyes, making him look troubled, as if something was weighing heavily on his mind. 'I hope I didn't disturb you,' she said, running her tongue over her dust-dry lips.

He picked up some wayward strands of her hair and tucked them behind her ear. 'You didn't disturb me,' he said. 'I often have trouble sleeping.'

She shivered in delight as his long fingers brushed and then lingered against the skin of her neck once he had secured her hair. 'You work too hard,' she said huskily. 'You drive yourself all the time. When was the last time you had a day off?'

He gave a rueful movement of his lips as his fingers found another few strands of her hair to toy with. 'I have a large corporation to run, Maya,' he said. 'Especially now, with my grandfather fading so quickly.'

'But surely Luca and Nic are helping you?'

He gently coiled her hair around his index finger. 'They are a great support and both work very hard but there are some things I just have to see to myself.'

'You didn't answer my question,' she pointed out. 'When did you last have a day to yourself?'

He let her hair unravel from his finger as his eyes came back to hers. 'I will take some time off once my grandfather passes,' he answered. 'Maybe we could go somewhere together if the doctor gives the all clear to travel. It could be like a second honeymoon.'

Maya traced her fingertip over the sculptured contour of his top lip, his dark stubble catching on her soft skin. 'If we lose this baby…'

He captured her finger and tenderly kissed the end

of it, his eyes still holding hers. 'We haven't lost it so far, *cara*,' he said. 'Hang on to that hope. We have come this far. Hopefully, we can this time around have what we both want.'

As his mouth came down to cover hers, Maya said a silent prayer that somehow what he said would be true, even though she was well aware that she wanted much more than he was prepared to give.

CHAPTER TEN

OVER the coming weeks Maya saw less and less of Giorgio. Salvatore's illness had progressed to the point where he needed around the clock care. Giorgio had to divide his time between keeping the intrusive press at bay, as well as seeing to his grandfather's affairs on top of his own workload, which was considerable at the best of times. Maya began to see for the first time since they had married that the frenetic fast-paced life he lived was not perhaps his choice, but rather something he did because so many people relied on him. It made her more committed to trying to support him in the background, making sure the villa was a comfortable and quiet refuge when he came home, sometimes well after she had gone to bed.

She was still getting used to being back at the villa. It was a different environment without the crew of household workers that had worked there previously. The new sense of space gave her time to think. She was too frightened to plan too far ahead, but she was content for the time being to support Giorgio as much as she could through the difficult time of facing his grandfather's passing. She even spent long hours with Salvatore in order to give some of the other family members a break. She enjoyed sitting there with the old man, chatting to him if and when he felt up to it, or simply reading the paper to him or from one of his favourite novels.

In spite of his long absences from the villa, Giorgio still shared Maya's bed at night. She looked forward to those passionate interludes, when he would silently reach for her, gathering her into his arms and showing her a world of sultry hot delights that made her flesh hum and sing for hours afterwards. He still refused to have penetrative sex, which she found frustrating, but she was hopeful now that she had passed the danger zone of her pregnancy he would soon change his mind.

She was now close to twelve weeks pregnant. She still could barely believe it. Even seeing the baby on the follow-up ultrasound she'd had earlier that week seemed like a dream. As each day passed she felt a fraction less terrified that this too would end in despair.

That Giorgio was thrilled about the progress of her pregnancy was unmistakable, but what was less certain was what he felt about her. To be fair to him, she understood he had a lot on his mind at present, so his air of distraction at times had probably very little to do with her but more to do with the stress he was dealing with. He was gentle and solicitous towards her. No one looking in from the outside would take him for anything but a loving husband, proudly awaiting the birth of his surprise baby.

Giorgio's family showed no signs of thinking anything different. Maya and Giorgio had joined them for dinner at Giovanna's invitation only the week before.

Although, of course, everyone was feeling rather subdued because of Salvatore's deterioration and because he was too unwell to join them downstairs, the event proved to Maya that the family took it for granted she was back in the Sabbatini fold and was not going anywhere in a hurry.

Bronte, Luca's lovely wife, was fast becoming a friend. Maya had offered to help her learn Italian and they had enjoyed a couple of sessions at the villa with little Ella joining in with much enthusiasm. Maya had loved being with the little toddler, who seemed to be blossoming as each day passed. Bronte too, who was fourteen weeks pregnant now and glowing with it, helped Maya to feel a little less worried that things would go wrong this time around.

The persistent and rather hideous nausea Maya was still experiencing, Bronte assured her, was a fantastic sign, similar to what Giorgio had said, which the doctor too had confirmed only that afternoon when she had gone in for a check-up.

Maya was sitting curled up with a book waiting for Giorgio to come home when she heard the front door of the villa open and close. Gonzo whined as if he sensed something was wrong even before Giorgio walked into the room.

Maya felt the book she was holding slide out of her hands; she barely registered the little thump as it landed on the carpeted floor at her feet. 'Giorgio?' Her voice came out as a whisper of dread.

His eyes looked hollow as they connected with hers.

'He's gone,' he said in a flat emotionless tone. 'He died two hours ago. He went very peacefully.'

Maya felt her lip quiver and her eyes filled with tears. She scrambled to her feet and half stumbled, half fell into his arms. She wrapped her arms around him tightly, as if she could take some of the pain away from him and carry it for him. 'I'm so sorry,' she said, struggling to keep her emotions in check. 'He was such a wonderful person. He will be missed so much.'

Giorgio rested his head on the top of hers, his arms going around her to hold her close. 'Yes, he will,' he said. 'But he wanted us to move on. He didn't want us to feel sorry for him or wallow in grief. He wanted us to live life to the full, like he did.'

If only life wasn't so capricious, Maya thought. Living it to the full was fine for some people, but once you had been hit from the left-field a couple of times it made one rather cautious about living in the moment.

Giorgio put her from him after a little while, still anchoring her with his hands curled around her upper arms. 'So how are you feeling, *cara*?' he asked. 'What did the doctor say? I am sorry I couldn't come with you. Did you get my text message? I got caught up with my grandfather's palliative care doctor. I couldn't really get away in time.'

Although Maya was a little surprised by his rapid change of subject, she was starting to see it was his way of coping, to move on with life as if nothing had happened. He would grieve but he would do so in private. 'Yes, I got your message and I totally understand. It was just a check-up, in any case. Everything is fine. Dr

Rossini thinks the nausea should settle in another few weeks.'

He smiled and placed his hand on her still flat belly. 'No one would ever know you are carrying my child in there,' he said. 'How soon before you will start to show?'

'Bronte said it might not show for another month or two,' she said. 'She said she was almost five and a half months before she did with Ella.'

'I think we should make an announcement to the press once my grandfather's funeral is over,' he said. 'Look at how much attention Luca and Bronte got over their love-child and then the wedding and now a second pregnancy. It's what people want to hear. They thrive on it.'

Maya frowned at him. 'But I thought you wanted to keep the press out of this for as long as possible?'

He dropped his hands from her and moved across to the bar area. He poured some iced water in a tall glass and handed it to her before he made himself a brandy and dry. 'My grandfather wanted the Sabbatini name to be associated with growth and success, not illness and death,' he said. 'We owe it to our investors and the staff and guests in all of our hotels to remind them life goes on, business as usual. The announcement of our much anticipated child will draw attention away from the family's loss at this time.'

Maya was incensed. She hated the thought of the press hounding her, chasing her, perhaps even putting her life and that of her baby in danger as they shoved and crowded her for a photo. 'So this is all a business strategy to you, is it?' she asked.

Giorgio took a deep draught of his drink before he answered. 'You are overreacting, as usual, Maya. I am merely saying we need to stay focused on the positive, not the negative. I manage a huge global corporation. I don't want anything to have a negative impact on it and nor did my grandfather. Those were some of the last words he spoke to me.'

Maya turned away, putting her glass down with a loud thud on the coffee table. 'I will not agree to have the news of my pregnancy splashed over every paper and gossip magazine in the country, if not all over Europe, just so you can make money out of it.'

'Maya—'

She turned on him like a snarling cat. 'Don't patronise me with that I'm-the-one-in-charge tone. You know how much I hate the intrusion of the press. It's one of the reasons our marriage crumbled.'

His mouth became tight-lipped. 'The reason our marriage crumbled was because you were not mature enough to face the reality that life doesn't always go according to plan. You acted like a spoilt child who couldn't have what she wanted right when she wanted it. You stormed out of our marriage pouting all the way.'

Maya's mouth dropped open in outrage. 'You're calling *me* a spoilt child? What about you, with your private jet and Lamborghini and Ferrari, for God's sake. You know *nothing* of what it's like to struggle. All your life you've had everything handed to you on a silver family crest-embossed platter.'

He put his now empty glass down. 'I am not going to be drawn into an argument with you. You are upset over my grandfather's death. I shouldn't have even brought up the subject of the press announcement.'

Maya refused to be mollified. She folded her arms and glared at him.

Spoilt child, indeed.

Pouting all the way out of her marriage.

What the hell did he mean by that? He would have divorced her as quick as a wink if it hadn't been for what he stood to lose in a settlement.

She watched as he poured himself another drink, a double this time. He wasn't a huge drinker, which made her realise with a little jolt that he was feeling his loss rather more deeply than he was letting on. He had said *she* was upset about his grandfather's death but, as usual, he had not said anything about how he was feeling.

'Giorgio…' She curled her fingers around each other, uncertain how to progress.

'Leave it, Maya,' he said, raising his tumbler to his lips.

She waited for a beat or two. 'How is your mother taking it?' she asked.

He didn't even bother to turn around to face her to answer. His left shoulder hiked up and down in a shrug. 'She is upset, of course. It will no doubt bring back the pain of the loss of my father, but she has her family around her. Luca's with her now and Bronte and gorgeous little Ella. She will be the best distraction for *Mamma*—for all of us, actually. Nic's due to fly in tomorrow. He's in Monte Carlo, probably gambling or sleeping with some wannabe starlet or both.'

'You disapprove of his lifestyle, don't you?' Maya asked after another little pause.

Giorgio turned around and looked at her, glass in hand. 'You think I have had every privilege and certainly, compared to you, that is indeed the case, but don't for a moment think I don't appreciate or value what I have been given as a birthright. Luca had to grow up and grow up fast when he almost ruined his own and Bronte's life. Nic has yet to learn to take responsibility for his actions. But I have a feeling he is about to.'

'Oh?' she asked. 'What makes you say that?'

He gave her a grim look. 'My grandfather talked to me briefly about his will. Nic is not going to like some of the terms, let me tell you. If he doesn't toe the line within a year he will be disinherited.'

Maya flinched in shock. 'Salvatore stated *that* in his will?'

Giorgio nodded and took another generous mouthful of his drink. 'The feathers are about to fly, or at least they will when Nic finds out when the will is read. If he wants to contest it he will have a lengthy and very expensive fight on his hands. I am hoping he won't go down that path. The press will make a circus of it, for one thing. Also, it could mean trouble for the Corporation if Nic defaults.'

'I'm not used to these sorts of things,' she said. 'When my mother died she hadn't even left a will. She didn't have anything to leave in it, even if she had gone to the trouble of writing one.'

Giorgio put his glass down on the bar. 'You must have missed her when she died so suddenly. You've hardly ever talked about it.'

Maya tried not to think of that time. She hated being reminded of her lonely childhood, how much of a burden she had been made to feel by her penurious great-aunt, how much she had longed for a cuddle or a word of praise and encouragement from a woman who loathed all forms of affection and who thought words of affirmation would unnecessarily inflate a child's ego.

Maya's school days had been the worst. Watching as all the other kids had one or both parents come to assemblies or end of school prize nights. Her great-aunt had not attended a single event. Eunice Cornwell didn't believe in competition of any sort, so when Maya had taken out the Headmaster's Prize for Outstanding Academic Achievement at her Leaver's Assembly no one had been there to see it.

'It wasn't a great time in my life,' Maya said. 'My great-aunt resented having me thrust upon her. I resented being there. I left as soon as I possibly could.'

'Poor little orphaned Maya,' Giorgio said, coming over to where she was standing so stiffly. 'No wonder you were attracted to me with my big family.'

'I was attracted to you, not your family,' Maya said.

He lifted the hair off the back of her neck, sending the nerves beneath her skin into a frenzy of delight. 'Ah, yes,' he said. 'And you still are, aren't you, *tesore mio*?'

'I can hardly deny it when I am currently carrying

the evidence in my belly,' she said in a wry tone. *Long may it continue*, she tacked on silently.

His other hand went to her abdomen, pressing against it gently but possessively. 'I want to make love to you,' he said, his voice deep and sexy and irresistible. 'Now.'

Maya felt her insides flip over. That dark smouldering look in his eyes sent her heart racing and when he traced a fingertip down over the curve of her breast, even though she was still fully dressed, she felt her nipple instantly engorge with blood. 'Are you asking me or telling me?' she said in a voice that wobbled with anticipation.

His head came down, his brandy-scented breath skating over her upturned mouth. '*Do* I need to ask, *cara*?'

She gave him his answer in actions not words. She met his mouth with hers, sliding her tongue to join his in a sexy duel that got more and more heated the longer it continued. She was breathless by the time he had her locked in his arms, her dress in a pool at her feet, her breasts bare and aching for his mouth. She gasped as his lips closed over her tightly budded nipple, the pleasure so acute she felt her senses spin out of control.

The passion became an inferno, consuming everything in its path. There was no time for moving upstairs, no time for lingering over kisses and caresses or murmuring sensuous promises.

Giorgio pressed her down to the carpeted floor, his body joining hers, covering her with his weight balanced on his arms. His mouth came back to hers, taking it in another steamy assault of the senses, thrusting and probing with his tongue in a delicious and erotic mimic of what was to come.

Maya writhed with want beneath him. She wanted him naked and slick with her moisture and his inside her. She wanted to feel that hard pumping of his body she had missed so much. She became totally wanton with her need. She clawed at his clothes, popping buttons and pulling out his belt from its loops like a madwoman on a mission.

He worked on her clothes with a little more finesse, but not much. He kissed each part of her body he exposed, his lips and tongue lighting fires all along her flesh. He feasted on her breasts, sucking and pulling, swirling his tongue around each nipple, making them pucker even further.

Maya took him in her hand, relishing the turgid potency of him. He quivered and throbbed and then tugged her hand off him, pressing her back down and entering her with a stabbing thrust that sent a shockwave of rapture throughout her body.

He immediately checked himself, retreating a little in case he had gone too deep, but she dug her fingers into his buttocks and urged him even deeper. He groaned and thrust again and again, harder and faster, his breathing becoming ragged, fine beads of perspiration springing up over his flesh and hers as she too felt her control slipping in the heat and fire of the moment.

The friction was just right, catching her swollen pearl of need, the secret heart of her that responded to him so wantonly. She arched her spine and gave herself up to the orgasm as it swept her up into its vortex, swirling and tossing her about like a ragdoll. She shook and quaked with the power of it, the reverberations of her body sending Giorgio into his own powerful release. She felt every muscle in his body tense in that split second before he finally unleashed his control. The quick hard pumps of his body spilling hotly into hers made her feel another wave of pleasure, her inner core pulsing with it until she was as limbless and sated as he.

Maya lay beneath him, her heart still hammering with the thrill of having him possess her totally. She didn't want to talk and spoil the moment. She wanted to cling to this special closeness for, even though she suspected it was more physical than emotional for him, for her it was all about the feelings she had for him, and that was the way it had always been. She couldn't separate the lust from the love like other people did. Even the night of Luca's wedding, when she had fallen into bed with Giorgio, it had been less about lust and more about love.

Fate had brought them back together, fate and circumstances that meant she would have to think very carefully before she took it upon herself to walk away again.

Sabbatini men played for keeps. Losing was not in their vocabulary. Giorgio's relationship with her had nothing to do with love. It was all about pride and ownership and continuing the blue-blooded line of the family.

But that might be the one and only thing Giorgio could not control, even though Maya dearly, longingly, prayerfully wished it were.

CHAPTER ELEVEN

THE funeral for Salvatore Sabbatini was large but the service was still deeply meaningful and poignant. Salvatore had lived a good life, a long life marked along the way with a lot of success and a measure of tragedy. Outliving his son Giancarlo was something he had grieved over in his own way, and when Maya saw the PowerPoint presentation Giorgio had put together of his grandfather's life she too, along with most of the other mourners, had to wipe tears from her eyes as she witnessed the moving sweep of his life, from that of a small child to his last days, holding his much anticipated great-grandchild Ella on his knee.

The celebration of his life continued at a private function in the Sabbatini hotel. It was mostly attended by family and close friends but somehow one or two members of the press had sneaked in. While Maya was watching everyone from the sidelines she suddenly found herself face to face with a large camera lens aimed at her.

'Signora Sabbatini,' the paparazzi man said, 'is it true you are expecting a child?'

Maya was caught off guard and, after too long a pause, mumbled, 'No comment.'

'Word has it the child could be that of Howard Herrington, the man you had a brief affair with during your estrangement from your husband. Everyone knows you and your husband had issues with fertility over the past few years. Do you have anything to say about that?'

Giorgio suddenly appeared at Maya's side, his expression infuriated beyond anything she had witnessed before. 'There is absolutely no truth in those rumours,' he said. 'The child is mine; there is no doubt about it and there never has been. Now, leave, before I ask Security to escort you from the premises.'

The journalist sloped off and Giorgio took Maya's elbow and led her to one of the vacant rooms off the main function room. He closed the door and looked down at her with concern etched on his features. 'Are you all right?' he asked. 'I thought you were going to faint for a moment there.'

Maya placed a shaking hand to her forehead. 'I should have been more prepared…I felt like a stranded fish, standing there with my mouth opening and closing before I could think of something to say.'

He rubbed the side of his face with one of his hands. 'I was hoping to avoid this,' he said. 'That's why I wanted to make a proper announcement before the press got in first with their stupid speculation. It's much harder to control the rumours when they come from unknown sources.'

Maya studied his brooding expression for a moment.

'There's no doubt in your mind that this is your child, is there, Giorgio?'

'No, of course not.' He pushed his hair back where it was falling forward. 'Not now.'

'What do you mean, "not now"?' she asked. 'Has something or someone confirmed my side of the story?'

His dark eyes met hers, holding them for a beat or two before he answered. 'I ran into your date, Howard Herringbone.'

Maya didn't bother correcting him this time. 'Ran into him?' she asked with a sceptical lift of her brows. 'I can't imagine under what circumstances you would...' she put her fingers up like quotation marks '... run into him.'

'All right, I admit it,' Giorgio said after a tense pause. 'I tracked him down and paid him a visit. He confirmed that you and he had met once for a meal that was set up by a mutual friend.'

Maya was beyond anger. She stood with her blood roaring in her ears at his audacity, at his lack of trust, at his arrogance and bullheadedness. 'So you didn't believe me,' she said through tight lips. 'You could only do that when you had confirmation from another source.'

'Think about it from my side, Maya,' he said. 'It would have been the perfect payback. You left me when I failed to get you pregnant. What else was I to think when I discovered you were carrying a child?'

'I didn't just leave you because you failed to get me pregnant,' she shot back. 'I left you because our marriage was dead.'

'Even so, you didn't exactly rush to tell me,' he said. 'I only found out by chance when I opened that drawer in search of a toothbrush.'

'I was going to tell you,' she said.

His expression was cynical. 'When? Like Bronte did to Luca? When the child was over a year old?'

Maya sprang to her new friend's defence. 'That was Luca's fault, not Bronte's. He was the one who cut her from his life without a single explanation as to why. He didn't trust her enough to tell her the truth about his situation.'

'Luca is a very private person,' Giorgio said. 'He didn't even tell his own family what he was going through.'

'I don't want to get into it,' she said. 'They have sorted it out now and are so much in love; how could anyone not be happy for them?'

'I *am* happy for them,' he said. 'I just know that Luca has missed out on his child's first year of life. No one can make that up to him or to us as his family. We were all cheated of that year. I would never forgive you the way he has done Bronte if you had tried to pull that kind of stunt on me.'

Maya glared at him heatedly. 'How could I have done that when up until now I have never even stayed pregnant longer than a measly six weeks?'

The air rang with the pain of her words, filling every large and small space of the room with its presence.

He took a step towards her. 'Maya…'

She warned him off by folding her arms tightly around her body. 'Don't make this any worse than it already is,' she said. 'You forced me to come back to you to give your grandfather peace in his last days but he's gone now. I don't have to stay with you any longer. You can't force me. I could pack my bags and leave you today and there's nothing you could do to stop me.'

A flash of anger fired in his gaze like the blast of a gun. 'If you leave me this time around, Maya, you will regret it for the rest of your life. I was too easy on you the first time around. I thought you needed space; I thought we both needed it. But this time the gloves will be off. I will take my child off you as soon as it is born and don't for a moment think I couldn't or wouldn't do it.'

Maya swallowed as his hateful words began to sink in. This was no longer a fight for his money, but for his child as well. He would do anything to keep both under his control. She was immaterial to him: just another piece on the chessboard of his life, to move around as he pleased. If he loved her wouldn't he just have said so to get her to stay with him?

'You are assuming, of course, that this child will be born,' she said in a voice she barely recognised as her own: it sounded hard and bitter and full of ice-cold contempt.

'The doctor is very confident you will deliver a perfectly healthy child this time,' Giorgio said. 'I want that child, Maya. Don't make me take it off you with a long drawn out divorce and custody battle. You should know by now I will not let you win.'

She threw him a flaying look. 'I know you are ruthless and heartless when it comes to getting what you want. You are prepared to lock yourself into a loveless marriage for God knows how many years just so you don't have to give me what I want.'

'It seems to me you don't even know what you want,' he threw back. 'You said you wanted a divorce but as soon as we were thrown together for a few hours you were back in my bed. Nothing's changed, Maya. You want me. I want you.'

Maya hated that her colour was high. She felt the shame of her capitulation to him all over again. She was so weak, so wanton when it came to this man. Why couldn't she have better self-control? 'How long do you think this lust fest is going to last?' she asked.

His coal-black eyes glittered as they challenged hers. 'It's lasted pretty well so far,' he said. 'In fact, if there wasn't a crowd of people just outside this door I would take you here and now and prove it.'

Maya felt her body respond with hot wires of need. Her skin broke out in goose bumps at the mere thought of him possessing her the way he had done the night of his grandfather's death. They had made love every night since, and yet each time it had transcended the prior experience, as if her body was only now coming to full sensual maturity. She had lost so many of her inhibitions; she had enjoyed his body in every way possible.

There was a knock at the door that shattered the sensual spell like a rock on a thin glass window.

Giorgio strode over to the door and tugged it open. 'Yes?' he barked curtly.

'Oh…sorry,' Bronte, Luca's wife, said, blushing. 'I was just looking for Jade Sommerville. I saw her briefly at the funeral but I haven't seen her since. I guess she must have left early or something.'

Giorgio muttered something about not keeping a head count on every guest and how he should not be expected to and, curtly excusing himself, strode out of the room.

Bronte looked across at Maya, who was still standing with her body so stiff it looked as if she were wrapped in cling film and couldn't move. 'Are you OK, Maya?' she asked.

Maya unpeeled her arms from around her body and let out a sigh. 'Sorry about Giorgio being so rude to you just then. He's had a lot on his mind, as you can imagine.'

'I know.' Bronte's voice was softly sympathetic. 'It's such a sad time for the family. And poor Giorgio's had to do so much for so long. No wonder he's a bit tetchy with everyone. But how are you holding up?'

'I'm fine,' Maya said, shifting her gaze a little.

There was a small but telling silence.

'Look, you can tell me if it's none of my business, but I couldn't help noticing things were pretty tense with you and Giorgio just now,' Bronte said. 'Is that just because of the stress he's been under or something else?'

Maya felt her chin start to wobble but quickly got it under control. 'We are having some teething problems, but no doubt we'll sort them out in time. I haven't exactly been the best person to be around just lately. I can't quite let myself believe this baby is going to make it.'

'Oh, Maya.' Bronte came over and hugged her close. 'You poor, poor darling. I know it's hard but you have to think positively. Soon you'll be showing and then I am sure it will feel much more real to you.'

Maya pulled back from the hug after a moment. 'I know; it's just I'm not sure how to handle Giorgio. The thing is, I have never known how to handle him. I can't get close to him, at least not emotionally. He won't let me.'

Bronte frowned. 'You still love him though, don't you?'

'That's the problem,' Maya said on another heartfelt sigh. 'I love him just as much, if not more than I did before.'

'But?'

Maya's eyes met Bronte's concerned ones. 'Giorgio is incapable of love, or at least of showing it.'

Bronte frowned. 'But he must have loved you once. He married you, didn't he?'

Maya's chin wobbled again and she bit down on her lip to steady it. 'Our marriage was not a romantic match, more of an expedient one.'

Bronte's brows went up. 'What on earth do you mean?'

Maya sighed heavily. 'Giorgio and I met just before his father had the accident. I fell in love with him, but he only married me because his family expected it of him, especially once things looked so grim with his father. His goal was to get married and have an heir and I stupidly agreed to it, hoping that one day he would fall in love with me, but of course he didn't. We made each other positively miserable, especially when it became pretty clear I wasn't going to fulfil my end of the arrangement in producing an heir and a spare on schedule.'

'Oh, Maya,' Bronte said again, clearly lost for words.

'We're only back together because of Salvatore dying and, of course, the baby,' Maya went on. 'If it hadn't been for this pregnancy, we would be apart now that Salvatore is gone. Giorgio was as keen to move on with his life as I was to move on with mine.'

Bronte's expression looked pinched with pity. 'Oh, dear... You surely don't think he has someone else? You know, like a mistress or something?'

Maya thought of that svelte lingerie model and pain sliced through her like the blade of a scimitar. 'I don't know...maybe...I hope not...'

Bronte put a gentle hand on Maya's arm. 'Do you want me to have a word with Luca about it to see if he can talk to Giorgio?'

Maya shook her head. 'No, please don't involve Luca or anyone else in this. Giorgio and I have to sort it out ourselves.'

'Give it time, Maya,' Bronte advised. 'A lot of stuff has happened over a short period of time. From what I've seen, Giorgio takes on a lot of the stress for other people. I guess that comes from being the oldest brother. Once things settle down a bit he might see things differently. He certainly looks and acts like he cares about you. Luca and I were only discussing it the other day. Giorgio is so protective of you, making sure you get enough rest and don't do too much. He was absolutely furious with us for allowing you to sit with Salvatore for several hours the week before he died—you know, the day I had my doctor's appointment? He said you were only to be allowed to take short shifts. I was quite frightened of him but Luca assured me it was because he really cares about you and the baby.'

The door opened and Luca came in carrying a fractious Ella. 'Ah, here she is,' he said, winking at Bronte. 'Here's Mummy.'

'Mum Mum,' Ella wailed piteously and reached out her little arms for Bronte.

Maya felt a wave of envy go through her. How she longed for a child of her own to do exactly that, not to mention a husband as loving and devoted as Luca was to Bronte.

'This young lady needs a sleep,' Bronte said, smiling ruefully at Maya. 'Do you want to go shopping with me tomorrow? I can come and pick you up. I found this great maternity boutique. There was a pink and white top and trousers with an expandable waistline that would look fabulous on you with your gorgeous colouring.'

Maya smiled. 'I would love that. I haven't got anything planned.'

'Great,' Bronte said, cupping Ella's sleepy head against her shoulder. 'I'll pick you up about eleven, OK?'

Maya watched as Luca put a loving arm around his wife as they left the room together, the bond of their child and the new one they were expecting cementing them together in a bond that was unbreakable.

The door had barely swung shut when it opened again, roughly this time, with a stormy-looking Nic striding in, ready for some sort of showdown. 'Oh, *scusi*,' he said, pulling up short when he saw her. 'I thought you were someone else.'

'Sorry to disappoint you,' Maya said, unable to remove the tartness from her tone in time.

Nic's expression lost some of its hardness. 'Look, Maya, I know you think I belong under a rock some place but, for Giorgio's sake, can we try and get along? I'm really happy about you being back together. Giorgio needs the stable influence. He's not been the same since you left him.'

'I might not be able to give him the family he wants,' she said. 'It's still early days.'

'You're doing a great job so far,' he said, his eyes flicking to her belly and back with a green-flecked twinkle in them.

'I'm really sorry about your grandfather,' Maya said to fill the awkward little silence.

The hardness came back into Nic's face, making him look older than his thirty-two years. 'That old conniving bastard has just tried to screw up my life,' he bit out. 'But I am not going to roll over for him or for anyone.'

'You sound exactly like your brother,' she said with a touch of wryness.

'Yeah, well, I'll take that as a compliment, even though right now I swear to God I could bloody his nose for him. I just bet he put the old man up to this.'

'Up to what?' Maya asked.

'Never mind,' he said, shoving open the door. 'See you around.'

CHAPTER TWELVE

GIORGIO was silent on the drive home and Maya refused to try and nudge him out of it. She was still a little angry with him, but even angrier at herself for not having the strength to call his bluff over his threats. She could leave him before the baby was born and spend the next six months just as miserable as the six months she'd spent when she left him the first time. But, for the baby's sake and her own, she decided to stay. She was just starting to feel the bloom of pregnancy everyone always talked about, the higher level of energy, the glow of the skin and the rush of hormones that made her feel gloriously alive as a woman. It would be crazy to jeopardise all of that by living in a rented flat with Gonzo, who would no doubt lounge about mirroring her misery every day.

Besides, this had been a tumultuous and very difficult time for the Sabbatini family. They were all feeling the loss of Salvatore and it would be selfish of her to complicate things at such a raw emotional time.

And then, of course, there was the fact that she simply didn't want to miss seeing Giorgio every day. She was only just beginning to understand his character. He often showed an air of aloof indifference when something was troubling him. In the past she had taken that as cold dismissal of what was important to her, but now she could see he needed a little more time to process things before he revealed what he felt about them.

Bronte's revelation about his reaction to her sitting with Salvatore for so long had surprised her. Giorgio had made no mention of it, although she seemed to recall he had employed another nurse soon after that day. But maybe that was because the baby was his main priority. It was the only reason their marriage was continuing, after all.

But, in spite of everything, Maya didn't want him to miss seeing their baby grow inside her. Bronte had told her a couple of weeks back how hard it had been to have no one by her side, apart from her mother, when she was carrying Ella. Bronte had longed for Luca to have been there, witnessing every subtle and not so subtle change in her body, as he was doing now for this new baby.

She placed her hand on her abdomen protectively, wondering if the baby could sense how much love she had for it, how much she longed for it to grow to full term and arrive safely. If will alone could achieve such a miracle, she felt she was in with a very good chance.

'Are you feeling all right?' Giorgio asked, glancing at her. 'You're not in pain, are you?'

Maya put her hand back in her lap with her other one. 'Is it the baby you're worried about or me?' she asked, longing for reassurance.

His mouth tightened as he turned the car into the driveway. 'I have a lot of worries in my life right now and you are certainly one of them,' he said.

'Thanks,' she said. 'That makes me feel a whole lot better.'

He blew out a breath as he turned off the engine and swivelled in his seat to face her. 'I am sorry for taking a hard stand with you over this issue of divorce you keep raising. It's not that I don't believe in ending a miserably empty marriage; I just think we could make things work for us if we stick at it.'

Maya looked into his eyes, wondering if she had the courage to ask him outright what his feelings for her were now. But then she wasn't sure she would believe him if he said he did love her. How easy would it be for him to pretend so she fell in with his plans?

Celebrity divorces were ugly. They were also very public and a lot of mud could get thrown back and forth. He would want to avoid it just as much as she would.

He reached out and brushed the back of his bent knuckles along the curve of her cheek in a faineant movement that sent all her nerves dancing in delight. 'I promised my grandfather I would look after you,' he said in a husky tone. 'You were like another grandchild to him. I think he saw you as a replacement of the grand-daughter he lost.'

Maya put her hand over his, holding it to her cheek. 'You never talk of her—of Chiara,' she said softly. 'I don't think I've even seen a photo of her.'

His eyes became shadowed and he pulled his hand out from under hers. 'She would have looked just like Ella,' he said, his hands gripping the steering wheel tightly, even though the car was not in motion. 'Luca showed me some photos of when Ella was the age Chiara was when she died. It was like looking at a mirror image.'

'It must have been a terrible time for you, finding her like that,' she said, imagining the tragic scene in her head and feeling sick with anguish for him.

There was a silence that lasted only a few seconds but it felt much, much longer.

'It was,' he said, his expression darkening as if he were walking back through to that tragic day in his mind. 'I went into her room and it was so silent, so terribly, eerily silent. And then I realised she was too still, too pale, waxy, just like a doll.'

Maya swallowed against the tennis ball of emotion that clogged her throat. 'Oh, Giorgio...'

'We should go inside,' he said, swiftly changing the subject. 'You have been on your feet way too long and I too am exhausted. It's been a hell of a long week.'

Maya followed him into the villa, glad of his supportive arm around her waist, the feel of that strong band of flesh reminding her of all the passion that simmered between them, even when they were angry with each other. He had opened up to her, just a little bit, just enough for her to see how deeply he felt about things even though he gave no outward sign of it. He was obviously trying to connect with her for the sake of their baby. It clearly wasn't easy for him. She had seen the struggle played out on his face as he had spoken of finding his baby sister and she loved him all the more for it.

Once inside, Giorgio turned her into the circle of his arms. 'Why don't you go upstairs and run a bath? I will join you in a few minutes. I have some calls and emails to see to first.'

Maya felt her heart trip in excitement. Sharing a bath with Giorgio was an experience that was totally unforgettable. They hadn't done it since their reconciliation but she knew it would be every bit as thrilling as the last time they had, if not more.

She was sitting soaking luxuriously in a deep pool of warm bubbly water when he came in. He was totally, gloriously naked. She feasted her eyes on his body: his broad chest with its dusting of coarse hair, his flat brown nipples, his even flatter abdomen, and lean hips and strongly muscled thighs, and the most intensely masculine part of him rising proudly between them.

He came over and stepped into the bath, sending a wave of rippling water over her partially submerged breasts. 'How's the water?' he asked with a smouldering look.

'Getting hotter by the minute,' she said with a deliberate arch of her spine to showcase her breasts, swollen with hormones.

His eyes went straight to them, his nostrils flaring like a proud stallion. 'You become more beautiful every day,' he said, sinking into the water and spreading his legs so she was encased between them.

Maya sat up to run her hands teasingly down his hair-roughened thighs, feeling him tense in response. She held his dark gaze, mesmerising him with the sultry promise of her eyes, knowing he would be throbbing with want within seconds of her reaching for him under the water. She tiptoed her fingers up and down his legs, stopping just short of his erection. 'You like that?' she asked.

'You know exactly what I like,' he said, lying back as she came forward.

Her breasts brushed along his chest, her nipples tingling with pleasure at the friction of his hair. Belly to belly, it was the most erotic sensation, feeling his desire for her burgeoning against her, seeking entry, aching for release, twitching with the need to do so as quickly as possible.

But she wasn't going to let him until she had teased him some more. She wanted him begging and she would not stop until he did so. So far, he had dictated all the terms in their relationship. Now it was her turn, using her feminine power to remind him that they were equals, at least when it came to physical desire. Sex was another way to connect, a deeply intimate way to show how compatible they were when other things were not taking centre stage.

She pushed a finger to the middle of his sternum, making him go down further into the water. 'Down, boy,' she said in a sexy tone. 'I'm not quite finished with you yet.'

'I thought you were tired,' he said in a kind of strangled voice.

She stabbed playfully at his chest again and fluttered her eyelashes at him. '*You* said that, not me. I am not in the least bit tired. In fact, I am just warming up.'

'*Dio*,' he groaned as she bent her head to his chest and licked each of his nipples in turn.

Maya kept going, lower and lower, slowly, tantalisingly

so, stringing out the anticipation, making him quiver with each sweep and glide of her tongue and gentle playful nip of her teeth. The water was too deep for her to do what she really wanted so she deftly pulled the plug, smiling as the sound of the water gurgling away filled the pulsing silence.

Giorgio's dark brows lifted. 'Bath's over?'

She was on all fours and coming dangerously closer. 'Definitely all over.'

'So…' he snatched in a breath '…what happens next?'

She gave him a come-hither look as she stood amongst the retreating bubbles, her hands sliding down over her breasts and belly and to the naked heart of her sex. 'I think you know what comes next.'

He did and he could barely wait.

He had never seen her in quite this mood before. She was like a sultry temptress, luring him into a sex game that was unlike anything he had experienced with her before. He was ready to come, just looking at her touching herself like that.

He got to his feet and followed her to the bedroom, not even caring about the wet slap of his footsteps on the marble floor and the bubbles that trailed in their wake.

He wanted her and he wanted her now.

Urgently, passionately and endlessly.

She turned at the bed and tilted one hip in a pose that said come-and-get-me. 'What are you waiting for?' she asked.

Giorgio came down on top of her, thrusting into her

moist core, making every hair on the back of her neck quiver in response. Her tight warm body clutched at him, drawing him into her, making it impossible for him to slow things down. He was rushing headlong into a climactic release, only just managing to control himself long enough to make sure her needs were met first. He played her with his fingers, the swollen heart of her so ready for him she gasped and cried out loud with the pleasure it evoked. Within seconds she was convulsing around him, triggering his own earth-shattering response.

Her fingers worked their way up and down his spine in the aftermath, her soft little caressing movements making his body react to her all over again.

Giorgio propped himself up on his elbows and looked down at her cheeks, which were flushed with pleasure. 'You know, when the baby gets bigger we won't be able to make love like this,' he said. 'We'll have to be a little more creative.'

He saw the flicker of worry in her eyes. 'Sometimes I feel like it's not happening…that it's all a dream and someone is going to wake me up and say you're not pregnant. There is no baby.'

He brushed the damp hair away from her face. 'I know you are, *cara*, but look how well you are doing. Everyone is remarking on how wonderful you look. You are positively glowing. It won't be long now and you will feel the baby moving inside you.' He placed his hand on her belly. 'I can't wait to feel him or her kicking its little feet.'

'Bronte said it will be another few weeks before I feel the first flutters of movement,' she said.

'You will tell me the first time you feel something, won't you?' he asked.

'Of course,' she said, lowering her gaze as she traced a finger over his collarbone.

In spite of everything, Giorgio was still worried she might leave him. He had left himself wide open for a financially crippling settlement by not organising a prenuptial agreement before they married. But, with his father's accident and then his rapid decline, there hadn't been time.

He wasn't comfortable making threats about taking sole custody, but he wanted this baby and he wasn't going to allow her to take it to the other side of the world, or in fact even to England, where he couldn't see it daily and have a positive influence on its life. He was not going to join the band of divorced fathers he knew, men who hardly ever saw their children, men who spent lonely weekends and Christmases and holiday periods while their children were with their mother and her new partner.

He wanted to give this child a stable and happy childhood. His childhood had been perfect until Chiara had died. It had taken him decades to be able to think of that time in his life without flinching. His parents had become shadows of themselves; it had taken years before they came out of the abyss of grief that had consumed them. But they *had* come out. They had worked at their marriage, even in spite of his father's couple of affairs, which had seemed more a product of Giancarlo's grief than any malicious desire to inflict hurt on his already suffering wife. Giorgio's mother had forgiven him and they had moved on and, up until his death, had enjoyed a close and loving relationship.

But then Giorgio's mother had always loved his father. She had loved him in spite of her pain over the loss of their daughter; she had loved him in spite of his betrayal with other women, she had loved him right to the end, when he had closed his eyes for the last time, lying in her arms.

Giorgio was not sure what Maya felt for him but he was almost certain it wasn't love. In the beginning she had been captivated by his wealth and lifestyle and the love she had spoken of back then seemed more a star-struck variety than the real thing. After the first year, she had stopped telling him she loved him, which more or less proved her feelings had not been genuine.

He was ashamed to admit he hadn't been in love with her when he asked her to marry him. It had been a convenient marriage for him, a way to secure his future. His world had been rocked by his father's accident and he had done what had been expected of him by marrying a suitable wife to continue the proud heritage he had been born into.

It had only been recently that he had thought long and hard about his feelings for Maya. They had been changing like the seasons: warm and cool, hot and cold. The experiences they had gone through had clouded things for him. He had shied away from the overwhelming emotions Maya demonstrated at times. It was the pattern of a lifetime and it had taken her leaving him for him to see it. But he knew that without the pressure of producing an heir and fulfilling everyone else's expectations he and Maya were amazingly compatible. Not just in bed, although that was wonderful and he constantly delighted in her body and how it made him feel, but it was more than that, much more. She had been a wonderful support to him through the agonising process of his grandfather's illness. She had sat for long hours reading to Salvatore and then, when she was not with him, she was at home at the villa, making sure things were in order when Giorgio got home exhausted from trying to juggle all the things he had to do. She quietly and diligently backed him up, offering comfort when he needed it, but also maintaining her new-found independence, not allowing him to dominate her, as he had done in the past.

Maya's voice interrupted his reverie. 'Do you think we should find out the sex of the baby on the next ultrasound?'

'Do you want to know or be surprised?' Giorgio asked.

'Haven't we had enough surprises?' she asked with a wry look.

He smiled and, leaning forward, pressed a soft kiss to the middle of her forehead. 'You continually surprise me, Maya,' he said and moved his lips down the side of her face until he got to her lips.

She moistened them in preparation, her eyes flaring with reawakened need. He lowered his head slowly, inch by inch, taking his time, waiting for that betraying little murmur of pleasure she gave when his mouth finally settled on hers.

No one could kiss like Giorgio, Maya thought. Not that she'd had a truckload of experience, but enough to know that when he kissed her there was no way it could ever be described as chaste and platonic. He kissed with sultry, steamy purpose, his need erotically apparent with every thrust and glide of his tongue inside her mouth.

When he moved his mouth to rediscover her breasts her back lifted off the bed in delight. She felt her nipples tighten to twin points of pleasure as his hot moist mouth enveloped each of them in turn. His hands cupped her feminine mound, teasing her with the so-close-but-not-close-enough presence of his clever, artful fingers.

She whimpered but he kept her hungry for him, holding her in his power, as she had done just minutes before.

Just when she thought she could stand it no longer, he gently but deftly turned her over onto her stomach, coming between her spread legs from behind in the most erotic position of all. There was a primal, earthy quality to it, a raw urgency that made her blood race like rocket fuel in her veins.

He entered her in one slick possessive thrust, a dominant surge of his body that spoke of his alpha status and her feminine submission to it. It was exciting, it was enthralling, it was everything she had hoped it would be. He had her coming apart in seconds, her whole body quaking with the tremors of release, until she was sweaty and sated, her flesh singing and tingling all over.

He waited until she had finished before he emptied himself, the action of his body pumping from behind with the brush of his hips against her sensitive buttocks making her feel a ripple of reaction all over again. She heard him groan deep in the back of his throat, signalling the supreme monumental scale of his pleasure.

Did he have this level of pleasure with anyone else? she wondered. The thought was unwelcome and intrusive, like a rat suddenly appearing under the table just as important dinner guests were to arrive. She couldn't make it go away; it nibbled at the edges of her consciousness, making her ill with the thought of how Giorgio could so easily have his cake at home and any number of gateaux on the side.

But how could she know without asking, and how could she ask without revealing how much it mattered to her?

CHAPTER THIRTEEN

When Maya woke the following morning she found Giorgio's side of the bed empty, which wasn't unusual since he was an early riser, but a sixth sense told her something was amiss.

She pushed back the covers and, slipping on a bathrobe, padded down the stairs. She heard him speaking on the phone from his study, which again was not unusual, even at this early hour, for he had business concerns all over the world in several different time zones. What was unusual was the way he was deliberately keeping his voice down, even though she could tell he was blisteringly angry.

He was speaking in English and it was undoubtedly to a woman.

As Maya listened her heart cramped with each word that was spoken, her fragile hopes of happiness dying an excruciatingly painful death.

'I told you never to call me on this number,' Giorgio was saying. 'Our association, as you call it, is over. I have other priorities now.'

The person on the other end of the line must have said something in return for he paused for a moment before continuing in the same harsh tone, 'I will deny each and every one of your claims. You have no evidence. Everyone will see it as nothing more than a money-making exercise on your part.'

Maya had heard enough. She slipped away and went into the kitchen, in desperate need of a glass of water to soothe her aching throat.

It was there that she saw the morning paper.

It was emblazoned with the features page headline: *Hotel Billionaire Giorgio Sabbatini Caught Out in Tell-all Exclusive by Lingerie Model Mistress.*

Maya's hand shook as she turned the pages to the section where there was a photograph of Giorgio and the lingerie model, called Talesha Barton, captured in a cosy-looking tryst in a nightclub. Talesha was everything Maya was not. She was buxom and tall, dark-haired and exotic-looking with wide almond-shaped eyes and a mouth that was impossibly full and sexy.

The tell-all story was full of saucy details of how the part-time model had met the estranged Giorgio Sabbatini and enjoyed a hot night of passion with him in a secret hideaway. 'He is an amazing lover,' the model was quoted as saying. 'He can go all night without a break. It was the best sex of my life.'

Maya swallowed against a tide of nausea and closed the paper, her whole body shaking with anger and despair and indescribable hurt.

Giorgio came into the room just as she turned from the bench. 'Maya?'

She threw the paper at him, the pages flying like sheets off a clothes line, landing all over the floor at his feet. 'You bastard,' she bit out through clenched teeth. 'You cheating, two-timing bastard.'

He frowned darkly. 'Now, wait just one damn minute,' he said, stepping over the debris of the paper on the floor. 'You surely don't think any of this rubbish is true, do you?'

Maya was close to hysteria. She could feel it bubbling up inside her; the pain and hurt and sense of betrayal was so acute it had nowhere to go but burst out of her. She felt so hurt, so crushed by his perfidy. And now it was all out in public, what he had been up to and who he had been up to it with. How would she ever hold her head up again? Would people always be looking at her and murmuring about what a naive fool she was to think he wouldn't return to his playboy form as soon as her back had been turned? How long was she to put up with this? Would there ever be a time when she would be free of this torture?

'How could you sleep with that…that…*tart*?' she asked.

His expression became stony. 'You are assuming I did actually sleep with her when you have nothing to base that on, other than what you have read in the paper. She was paid a lot of money for that fairy story and I swear to God that's all it is.'

'Oh, please.' She rolled her eyes in disdain. 'You were photographed with your arms around each other.'

'If I recall, so were you with your "date",' he returned.

Maya stiffened her shoulders. 'I told you nothing

happened. Someone took a photo that looked far more intimate than it was.'

'Likewise,' he said. 'Although I admit I did go out with her a couple of times and I considered taking it further but I decided against it. I let the press make what they wanted of it at the time. I was angry at you for leaving me so I didn't really care if you read about it at that point. Now it is different.'

'Because you want it all, don't you, Giorgio?' she said bitterly. 'You want the obedient, compliant little wife at home nurturing your children while you have your bit on the side, just like your father did.'

His jaw went rock-hard and his lips white-tipped at the corners. 'Keep my father out of this,' he said. 'My mother forgave him a long time ago for his fall from grace. It is their business, not ours. And he is no longer alive to defend himself, in any case.'

'Your mother was a fool to take him back,' Maya said. 'But maybe, like you with me, he didn't give her a choice. Did he blackmail her back into his life? Or was it the fact that she had three young sons to bring up all on her own that prevented her from leaving?'

Giorgio raked his hand through his hair. 'You have no idea what it was like for them. They lost their little girl, their much adored only daughter. It broke them. My mother grieved and grieved until she was so heavily sedated by the family doctor she couldn't function. I had to step in so many times to help look after my younger brothers, to feed them and bathe them and put them to bed when the nanny left without notice over something my mother had said in a moment of despair.' He stopped briefly to draw breath.

'My father couldn't cope. He had a hotel business to run. My grandfather and grandmother did what they could but no one could do anything to take away the pain. I lived with the fear of losing my mother, if not my father as well. I was convinced they didn't want to live any more. I had to do everything in my power to keep them strong, to keep the family together.'

Maya listened without interrupting. It seemed that each time he spoke about his baby sister he told her a little bit more of that tragic time. His gradual opening up to her helped her to understand more about his emotional distancing, the way he found excessive displays of emotion so off-putting. He'd had to be strong for everyone; he'd had to keep his emotions in check while everyone around him was falling apart.

'And then finally the cloud started to lift,' he continued. 'In an ironic way, I think it was my father's affairs that snapped my mother out of her depression. She knew she had to carry on, to do what she could to rebuild their relationship, which had been so happy before Chiara died.'

'I'm sorry,' Maya said softly. 'I didn't understand how hard it was, for you particularly. You were so young to be looking after everyone like that and feeling so responsible for them all.'

He looked at her with a grim expression on his face. 'Marriage takes a lot of work, Maya,' he said. 'Even good ones can have bad things happen to them. It is worse for people who live in the spotlight as everything we go through is reported in the press, often incorrectly.'

She eyeballed him, challenging him to tell the truth and nothing but the truth. 'Did you sleep with that model?'

It was a moment before he spoke.

A long moment.

'I am ashamed to say I fully intended to,' he answered. 'But when it came to the point of doing so I decided it wasn't the best course of action. Clearly, that ticked off Talesha Barton so her little payback was to have my reputation besmirched and my marriage put on the line for the second time.'

Relief made Maya feel giddy. She believed him because he had been honest, almost too honest. He had admitted how close he had been to having an affair, which, on reflection, she realised he'd had every right to have, considering they were officially separated at the time. 'Are you going to do anything about the story she gave to the press?' Maya asked. 'Will you ask for a retraction of it or take legal action against her or the paper?'

'I will get my legal team on to it,' he said. 'The sooner this is nipped in the bud the better. If the woman in question calls you, do not talk to her. Just hang up the phone. This is about money; it's not about anything else.'

A little bit like our marriage, Maya thought sadly.

He came over and tipped up her chin with his finger. 'I can't promise you the press won't target me again, or that some other woman I once dated before I met you won't see a chance to make money out of it and do so. All I can promise is that I will look after you and our baby, to build the family we have both always wanted.'

Maya decided to put herself out on an emotional limb. 'If I was to lose this baby, will you still want our marriage to continue?'

He frowned as if the question annoyed him. After all, it wasn't just the baby he wanted. He wanted to keep his fortune under his control and a costly divorce was hardly going to allow that.

'There are plenty of happy marriages around without children,' he said at last. 'Anyway, we have time on our side. We can have another round of IVF or even consider adoption.'

'Isn't love a prerequisite for a happy and fulfilling marriage?' she asked, stepping a little further out on that precarious emotional limb.

His eyes gave nothing away; they were dark and unfathomable. 'Like this baby, it will be a bonus if it happens,' he said. 'You claimed to love me once; perhaps you will find it possible to do so again, but maybe with a little more maturity this time.'

'You think I wasn't mature enough to know what love was back then?' Maya asked, frowning at him.

'You were blindsided, Maya,' he said. 'You said it yourself. What girl could resist the designer clothes, the holidays, the luxury villas and hotels?'

'Oh, for God's sake,' she said in frustration. 'I only said that to annoy you. I wasn't the least bit impressed by your wealth, well, maybe just a little bit in the beginning. I fell in love with you, not your money or your lifestyle. I just wanted to be with you, for who you were as a person.'

He looked at her for a heartbeat or two. 'Do you even know who that person is now?' he asked.

Maya looked into his eyes. 'I would if you would let me,' she said softly.

'I want to be the sort of person who can make you happy, Maya,' he said, touching her cheek again. 'But I am not good at showing emotion. I don't feel comfortable leaving myself open to possible hurt.'

'But don't you see you can't go through life not loving or needing anyone?' she asked. 'What sort of parent will you be if you can't show how you feel?'

'If you are suggesting that I will not love this child, then you don't know me at all,' he said. 'I would give my life for it, even now.'

'And what about me?' she dared to ask. 'Would you give your life for me?'

He took her by the upper arms and held her firmly, his eyes tethering hers with smouldering purpose. 'I have already given up my life for you, Maya,' he said. 'I have agreed to resume our failing marriage, haven't I? I could have walked away and started anew with someone else, but I didn't.'

'You know that's not what I am asking,' she said, holding his gaze as steadily as she could.

'Sometimes you ask too much, Maya,' he said, dropping his hold as if she had grown too hot to handle. 'I have things I need to see to—some business. I will be away for most of the week.'

Maya frowned. 'You're going away?'

He gave her an impatient look. 'I have a large corporation to control, Maya, you know that. My grandfather's death has intensified the workload. I have meetings in three different countries and long hours of paperwork and figures to trawl through.'

She dragged at her lip with her teeth, not sure whether she should reveal her vulnerability to him or not, but in the end she went for broke. 'But what about me?' she asked. 'I don't want to stay here by myself. Can't I come with you?'

His expression became shuttered. 'I think it is best that you stay here where you are close to the doctor you know and feel comfortable with. Dr Rossini is just minutes away if you feel worried about anything. Besides, the travelling might be too much for you. I am going to be locked away in meetings, in any case. I won't have time to spend with you.'

Maya felt hurt that he obviously didn't want her to be with him. 'Fine.' She folded her arms, not even caring that her bottom lip pushed out in a pout. 'No doubt I'll find something to do to entertain myself.'

'Maya, the press attention here is bad enough,' he said. 'But they are like jackals after a meal everywhere else. I don't want you to be harassed by them.'

'I can handle the press,' she said, glaring at the newspaper that was still lying all over the floor.

His brows moved together. 'I don't want you speaking to the press under any circumstances; do you understand?'

She raised her chin and gave him an arch look. 'Are

you worried I might sell out to them and tell the truth about how our reconciliation really came about?'

Anger flared in his dark gaze. 'If you do that you will regret it, Maya,' he said. 'I will make sure of it. You will not just be hurting me but my family as well. Do you really want to risk everything for a cheap shot at me?'

Maya held his burning gaze for as long as she could, but in the end she had to lower her eyes from his to stare at the floor. 'Of course I'm not going to speak to the press,' she said on an expelled breath. 'Surely you know me better than that.'

He tipped up her chin again with the blunt tip of his finger. He looked into her eyes for a long moment, his gaze deep and dark and inscrutable. 'Sometimes I wonder if I have ever known you,' he said ruefully. 'The real you, I mean.'

Likewise, Maya thought as his lips came down and pressed against hers.

CHAPTER FOURTEEN

MAYA had almost forgotten about her shopping date
with Bronte. She suddenly heard Gonzo barking and
then realised it was right on eleven o'clock.

She opened the door and Bronte immediately swept
her into a tight hug. 'Are you OK?' she asked. 'Oh, my
God, that awful, hideous story in the paper.' She pulled
back to look at Maya. 'You didn't believe a word of it,
did you?'

Maya bit her lip, uncertain of how to answer.

'Giorgio would not lie to you, Maya,' Bronte said.
'Luca told me how his brother's word is his bond. If he
said he didn't sleep with that woman, then he didn't.'

'He was going to,' Maya said, feeling the hurt all over
again.

Bronte looped her arm through one of Maya's. 'But
he didn't and that's the main thing. There are women
out there that are predators. They see rich and powerful
men as prizes to be claimed. Giorgio is too smart to let
himself be taken in by a trashy little gold-digger like that.
Give him some credit. He wants your marriage to suc-
ceed. He wouldn't do anything to jeopardise it now.'

Maya gave her a rueful smile. 'You seem to know

him better than I do and you only just met him a couple of months ago.'

'Ah, yes, but I know Luca and he's cut from the same cloth,' Bronte said. 'Now, let's go shopping. I have left Ella with Giovanna but I don't want to tire her too much. She is still very sad over Salvatore's death. How is Giorgio taking it?'

'He hasn't said much,' Maya said, thinking of how Giorgio had acted in the week since his grandfather's death. 'It's business as usual for him. That has always been the way he handles things. I think he grieves in private, however. In fact I know he does. He's away now for the next few days.'

'Did he tell you where he was going?'

Maya shook her head. 'No, and I didn't ask. All I know is he didn't want me to go with him.'

Bronte frowned. 'Maybe he didn't want to tire you with long hours of travelling. Living out of hotels, even Sabbatini ones, can be exhausting when you are pregnant.'

Maya shrugged. 'I guess…'

Bronte touched her on the arm. 'But you really wanted to be with him, didn't you?' she asked.

Maya bit down on her lip again, this time trying not to cry. 'I just want him to love me. Is that so very much to ask?'

'How do you know he doesn't love you?' Bronte said. 'There are lots of ways of saying it, other than in words. I know the words are important—I need to hear them too—but some men are just not comfortable revealing how much they love someone. It's a guy thing.'

'Does Luca tell you he loves you?'

'Yes, but he didn't until we got back together. Be patient, Maya. A few weeks ago, you were head to head with Giorgio in an acrimonious divorce. He's not going to let you get any power over him by admitting how much he needs and loves you. You might take it upon yourself to walk away from him again. No man in his right mind would lay himself open to that happening, especially a Sabbatini. You know how impossibly proud they all are.'

Maya knew what Bronte said was right, but she still didn't have the confidence to believe that Giorgio loved her the way she longed to be loved. All she could do was hope that by sharing the bond of a living child he would one day tell her what he felt, if anything other than lust.

The shopping expedition was a great success, so much so that Bronte insisted she come back to their villa for the rest of the afternoon. The afternoon drifted into the evening and then, because Luca was also away on business just for that night, Maya decided to stay on for dinner with Bronte rather than spend the evening alone at Giorgio's villa.

One of the staff drivers took her home just before ten p.m. and, as she opened the door, she could hear Gonzo howling because the phone was ringing incessantly.

She dropped her shopping bags on the floor and, giving the dog a quick reassuring ruffle of the ears as she moved past, she snatched up the phone. 'Hello?'

'Do you have any idea of how worried I have been

about you?' Giorgio raged at her, his voice tight with anger. 'Where the hell have you been and why haven't you got your mobile with you? I've been calling it all bloody day and night.'

Maya grimaced as she remembered how she'd turned it to silent when she and Bronte had lunched in a High Street restaurant. She had forgotten to turn it back to the ringtone. 'Sorry about that,' she said. 'I went shopping with Bronte. I went back to spend the rest of the evening with her at Luca's in London. My phone was on silent.'

'Don't ever do that again,' he said. 'I thought something must have happened to the baby.'

Maya suppressed her instinctive retort and, taking a calming breath, said, 'The baby is fine. I had a lovely day. I bought my first maternity outfit.'

There was a long drawn-out silence.

Finally Giorgio broke it but his voice sounded creaky. 'What colour is it?'

'Pink and white,' Maya answered. 'I don't really need it yet, but Bronte talked me into it.'

'It's good you have her to spend time with,' he said. 'I just wish you had told me your plans ahead of time.'

'I forgot all about her offer to take me shopping,' Maya said. 'Anyway, why should I tell you where I am going when you don't tell me anything about where you are going?'

'I told you I am on a business trip.'

'You didn't tell me where.'

'I am in Prague at the moment, I will be in Lyon in France tomorrow and the day after I am going to New

York. I will be back by the weekend. There is a charity ball at the hotel on Saturday night. I would like you to accompany me, if you're feeling up to it, of course.'

Maya gave her assent and, after another little silence, said, 'Bronte and Luca are going to the villa at Bellagio this week, just for a couple of days. They invited me to come along. Would you mind? I will be back in time for the ball.'

'Of course I don't mind,' he said. 'In fact, I think it would be good for you.'

There was another silence.

'Gonzo misses you,' Maya said softly.

'I miss him too.'

'Do you miss me?' she asked, kicking herself for being so transparent.

'I miss having you in my bed,' he said in a smoky tone.

Maya felt her insides flip over with longing. 'I miss that too,' she said.

'Maya...' he began, but then paused for so long she wondered if he had changed his mind about what he was about to say.

'What?' she prompted.

'Nothing,' he said. 'Just be safe while I'm away, OK?'

'I'll be fine,' she said, squashing her disappointment that he just wouldn't say what she most wanted to hear.

Maya had fed Gonzo after their return from Bellagio with Luca and Bronte and Ella and was about to unpack her small bag when she heard Giorgio's car pull into the villa grounds. Her heart leapt at the deep throaty sound. Gonzo gave a joyful bark and bolted down the stairs. Maya followed at a more leisurely pace, not wanting to show such blatant enthusiasm until she was more certain of where she stood with him.

Giorgio looked up from patting the dog when she came down the staircase. '*Cara*,' he said, smiling, 'you are positively glowing. Did you have a good time with Luca and Bronte?'

'I had a wonderful time,' she said, lifting her face for his kiss.

She tasted of strawberries and he wanted to keep kissing her until she was beneath him, begging for the release he had been dreaming of giving her the whole time he had been away. 'I have something for you,' he said, picking up the packages he had brought in with him from the car.

Her grey eyes flicked to the bags nervously. 'But I don't need anything,' she said. 'I have too many clothes as it is.'

'It's not clothes,' he said, 'or at least not clothes for you.'

She took a step backwards when he held the first bag out for her to take. 'No,' she said. 'No, Giorgio, take it away. Take it all away.'

Giorgio frowned. 'What's the matter, Maya? It's just stuff for the baby. I bought this sweet teddy bear; let me show you.' He bent down to pull it out of the tissue wrap but by the time he'd straightened Maya had turned on her heel and stalked out of the foyer.

He picked up the bags and followed her into the *salone*, his frown tightening when he saw that she had gone out of the French windows and to the furthest edge of the balcony.

He felt the all too familiar panic seize him, the perspiration starting to pop out of his pores as he looked at her holding onto the balustrade, her ramrod-stiff back turned towards him.

'Maya, come in here and talk to me,' he commanded.

She turned and, leaning on the balustrade, sent him a challenging glare. 'Why don't you come out here and talk to me?'

He clenched his teeth together, sure he would be spitting out tooth enamel dust for weeks hence. 'Get the hell away from the edge of that balcony,' he said, the perspiration dripping down now between his shoulder blades.

She continued to challenge him with her stony expression. 'You will have to come and get me because I am not coming in until you get rid of those bags and everything in them.'

Giorgio felt like scratching his head in bewilderment. He had spent a fortune on baby goods, he had shopped when he should have been working but he had enjoyed every minute of it. He had trawled through baby wear shops instead of through the company's figures. He had bought a train set for if it was a boy and fluffy animals and dolls for if it was a girl, and he had even ordered a make-it-yourself crib set that was being delivered from the States. He couldn't wait to teach himself how to assemble it and varnish it. He couldn't wait to get started on making a nursery. He now regretted redecorating the previous one. But Maya hadn't gone in there for years and at the time he'd been glad to have it removed, as it had only reminded him of his failure.

'Maya, this is ridiculous,' he said, holding out a hand to her. 'Come inside and let's discuss this like adults.'

She shook her head indomitably. 'Get rid of the bags. Now.'

He swore viciously and spun around, snatching up the bags and taking them to one of the storage cupboards in the foyer.

He came back in, relieved beyond belief to see her now back in the *salone*, but her face was still rigid with anger. 'Do you want to tell me what's going on?' he asked.

Her grey eyes rounded with hurt. *'How can you ask that?'* she said, her chin starting to wobble.

Giorgio still didn't get it. He was trying to but her reaction didn't make any sense to him. He was trying to be a good husband. He was trying to be the sort of involved father-to-be that he knew young mothers these days wanted and needed. 'Maya, tell me what's upset you. I am not good at reading between the lines. I deal with facts and figures: concrete things, not abstract ones.'

Her eyes were filling with tears as she faced him. 'Do you have any idea of what it's like to come home to a fully prepared nursery when you've just lost the baby you longed for with all of your heart? *Do you?'*

Giorgio swallowed what felt like a coil of barbed

wire. But he didn't answer. He couldn't. The words were somehow stuck in amongst those cruel barbs, scraping his throat, tearing at him with those awful dagger-like teeth.

'Four times,' she said, holding up four slim shaking fingers. 'Four times I did exactly that. I came home to teddy bears and toys and Babygro suits and b—booties I'd knitted myself. I felt such a fool, such a failure. I felt I had jinxed the baby's future by assuming too much too soon. I am not going to make that mistake again. *Never.* Not until I hold this baby in my arms am I going to buy a single item and nor will I let anyone, most of all you, buy them for me.'

Finally Giorgio found his voice. '*Cara*, I am so sorry. I should have thought.' He swallowed and lifted his hand to rake through his hair but it was shaking so much he let it drop uselessly by his side. 'I can't believe how stupid I have been. I should have known you felt this way. I was trying to be positive but it's not what you need right now, is it? It's not what you needed before either. What you needed was someone to meet you where you are emotionally.'

She nodded on a broken sob as his arms came around her to hold her close. He held her like that for long painful minutes, his own eyes moist with burning tears of regret of how badly he had handled everything.

No wonder she hated him.

No wonder she kept threatening to leave him.

He had not shown her how deeply he felt for her, for what she had gone through, for what she was *still* going through, with the uncertainty she felt was hanging over

her with this pregnancy, even though the doctor had
reassured her that everything was going according to
plan.

For Maya, given what she had been through, she
could not allow herself to relax until she was holding
that baby. It was less than twenty-five weeks until she
could do so, but that was a lot of days of worrying to
get through.

It was going to be a long wait, for both of them.

'Maya,' he said, holding her in the circle of his arms,
his eyes meshing with hers. 'Forgive me for being so
insensitive to your needs. Let me try and make it up to
you. I am not sure how I can, but I am going to try.'

She gave him a weak smile but her eyes were still
shadowed with sadness. 'It probably sounds so supersti-
tious to someone like you who deals with solid evidence,
but I just can't help it. I don't want anything to steal this
chance of happiness from me. I have wanted to be a
mother for so long. I look at Bronte and I feel so envious.
I look at every woman with a child or two or three and
feel like screaming with frustration that I haven't been
able to do this one thing that just about everyone takes
for granted.'

'We will get through this, Maya,' he said, his fingers
encircling her wrists, his thumbs stroking the sensitive
skin underneath.

'You are always so confident of getting what you
want,' she said with a little downward turn of her
mouth.

'I haven't always had everything my way,' Giorgio

said, thinking of how he'd felt the day he had found her note.

He had immediately switched off his feelings, as he did in times of stress. He had operated like an automaton, going through the motions as if the divorce was an annoying business deal he had to negotiate his way through. But on the inside he'd been screaming with frustration and injured pride. He had failed and the world was about to witness it and there had been nothing he could have done to stop it. He had cringed every time he had seen it mentioned in the press. His shipwrecked marriage had become gossip fodder, lining the pockets of unscrupulous journalists who wanted sensationalism, not the truth.

'You get your way most of the time, though,' Maya said. 'Like getting me back into your life, for instance. You weren't going to take no for an answer, were you?'

'That is true,' he said, bringing her hands up to his mouth, kissing both of them in turn. 'But then, that is where you belong, is it not?'

Maya knew there was no point in answering to the contrary. Instead, she lifted her mouth to meet the descent of his and gave herself up to the dream that, this time around, everything would work out the way she wanted it to.

CHAPTER FIFTEEN

THE charity ball was a huge affair that involved Giorgio making a speech about the work he was committed to doing for an orphanage he had set up in Africa.

Maya listened with rapt attention. She'd had no idea he had been involved in such a life-changing project for the little ones she saw on the PowerPoint presentation he had prepared.

Her heart ached for the tiny, soulful, dark-eyed infants who appeared on the screen. They had lost their parents through civil war and would have had no chance to survive if it hadn't been for the philanthropic efforts of people like Giorgio and his team of dedicated volunteers. The children were being lovingly cared for as they awaited adoption. They were being educated and had toys and clothing and special outings that would not have been possible without the enormous amount of time and commitment, not to mention money Giorgio had put in.

It made Maya feel she had been pathetically ungrateful for what she had in her life. Sure, she hadn't been able so far to have a baby, but there were literally millions of parentless infants in the world who would give anything to be loved and nurtured by someone who cared enough to give them a second glance.

She decided then and there that she would join Giorgio in his efforts to support those motherless and fatherless children; she would do anything to help them get a proper start in life.

He came back to their table and, now that the band had started its next bracket of songs, he asked her if she would like to dance.

'I would love to,' she said, slipping her hand into the warmth of his.

She went into his arms as if she had never been away, her steps falling into time with his as naturally as a professional ballroom dancer.

After a few head-spinning turns on the floor, she looked up at him with love and respect shining in her eyes. 'Why didn't you tell me about the orphan charity? I had no idea until now you were the sponsor behind it all. I had heard of it many times over the last few months, but I didn't for a moment think you were the one who had started and funded it.'

He expertly turned her away from a camera that was intent on taking a picture of them. 'I got to thinking about your childhood, how you had no one but an elderly spinster aunt to take you in when your mother died. It struck me that there are countless children in the same, if not worse circumstances. I decided if I couldn't have children of my own, I would do something for the ones who were already here but with no one to take care of them. It has been the most fulfilling enterprise of my life. Nothing compares to it. To see all those little faces light up when I fly in with gifts and toys and clothing is indescribable. I feel like a father to thousands.'

Maya was so touched she felt her eyes fill with tears. 'I feel so proud of what you have done. Can I come with you some time and meet the children?'

His hands tightened protectively. 'You, young lady, are going nowhere until this baby is born. Do you understand?'

'But Giorgio, I want to be a part of all of this,' she said. 'I need to be a part of it.'

'Then you will be a part of it, but on my terms,' he said. 'I want you to be safe for the rest of this pregnancy. I am not putting you at risk, taking you to a war-torn country with inadequate medical help.'

'If I wasn't currently pregnant, would you let me come with you?' she asked.

Giorgio frowned at her for a long moment before he finally answered. 'No, I would not.'

'But why?' she asked.

'Come on.' He took her by the hand and led her off the dance floor.

'Where are we going?' Maya asked.

'We're going home,' he said, barely pausing long enough to get their coats from the cloakroom.

Maya sat in the back of the limousine with Giorgio sitting stiffly beside her. He was looking out of the window, his fingers splayed out on his thighs, his jaw so tight it looked as if he was grinding his teeth.

'What's wrong?' she asked.

'Nothing is wrong,' he said, still with his gaze averted.

'Giorgio, I don't understand why you're so edgy all of a sudden,' she said. 'All I asked was to come with you some time in the future.'

He turned and looked at her with an intractable expression. 'It's out of the question. I absolutely forbid it.'

'It's about the baby, isn't it?' she said, resentment building inside her. 'You don't want anything to happen to the baby.'

'Of course I don't want anything to happen to the baby,' he said. 'Neither do you.'

Maya retreated into a frosty silence as their driver took them back to the villa.

Once they were back and alone at the villa, Giorgio tossed his coat over the back of the nearest sofa before he faced her. 'I know you think all I am interested in is having an heir,' he said. 'When I look back, I can see how you came to that conclusion. I haven't exactly given you any feedback of what I feel about you, apart from the obvious, of course.' His eyes flicked to the slight swell of her belly pushing against the satin of her dress.

Maya felt her heart slip sideways in her chest as his dark eyes met hers again. 'There is nothing wrong with wanting to have children,' she said. 'It's what I want too.'

He shifted his mouth in a rueful manner. 'You deserve much better than I can give you, Maya. I look at Luca and Bronte and how they are so open with their feelings for each other and I feel as if I have short-changed you. I married you for all the wrong reasons and then when you left me I let you go.' He rubbed at his cleanly shaven jaw and added with a heavy frown, 'I can't believe I did that.'

Maya swallowed to clear her blocked throat. 'We were both so unhappy, Giorgio,' she said. 'There was no point in carrying on. You didn't love me and I didn't—'

'Don't say it,' he said before she could finish.

She frowned. 'Don't say what?'

'I don't want to hear you say you no longer loved me,' he said, his throat rising and falling as he too swallowed tightly. 'I don't think I can bear hearing you say that. Not now.'

'I wasn't going to say that,' Maya said. 'I have always loved you. I know you think I was star-struck and immature and maybe I was—immature, I mean. In fact I am sure I was. I didn't take the time to understand you, to listen to what you didn't say rather than to what you did. I think you care about things a lot more than you let on. I see the way you care for your family. You do that out of love, not duty. I love that about you, that you always put others' needs before your own.'

Giorgio moved to close the distance between them, taking her hands in both of his. 'How can you still love me even though I have let you down in so many ways?'

Maya smiled, even though tears were falling from her eyes. 'I think we both let each other down,' she said. 'We didn't talk about what we were feeling. I always blamed you for that, but I can see now how I should have been more sensitive to what you were going through. You felt just as disappointed and sad when I lost our babies but you covered it up to protect me, just like you do with your family. You bear the brunt of everything to protect those you love.'

He pulled her close, holding her so tightly Maya felt imprinted on his body, but it was right where she wanted to be. 'I love you, *cara*,' he said. 'I know you might not believe it, but I do. I am deeply ashamed of not loving you when I married you, but in a way it was only in marrying you that I really came to know you and how you made me feel.'

He held her from him to look down at her upturned face. 'You tried so very hard to please me. You worked much harder at our marriage than I did. I arrogantly assumed everything would go according to plan and when it didn't I felt such a failure. I couldn't make you happy, I couldn't give you a baby, I couldn't do anything to make things right. And when you wanted out I let you go when I should have fought to get you to change your mind and try again.'

'Oh, darling,' Maya said, wrapping her arms around his waist. 'We both made silly mistakes. But we're together again now.'

He stroked her face adoringly. 'Yes, but only because of a chance encounter.' He grimaced and added, 'What if I hadn't asked you to come up to my room that night after Luca and Bronte's wedding to talk about the divorce? What if you had told me to go to hell instead? We might have missed this chance. We might have wrecked both of our lives.'

Maya nestled up closer. 'I only went up to your room

because I couldn't help myself. I missed you so much. I guess that was why I kept making such a fuss about sharing Gonzo. He was the final link with you that I didn't want to let go.'

He looked serious again as he cupped her face with his hands. 'Were you really going to go to live in London?' he asked.

Maya nodded. 'I had come to the point where I thought the only way to get over you was to get away. Even without Gonzo, there were almost constant reminders in the press of what you were doing. I couldn't take it any longer.'

Giorgio dropped his hands from her face so he could hug her close again. 'Yes, well, let me tell you, you would not want to have been a fly on the wall when I saw that article about you and that Herringbone guy,' he said. 'I swore and ranted and carried on for days until no one could bear to be around me. Quite frankly, I couldn't stand to be around myself.'

Maya smiled as she leant her cheek into his chest. She didn't bother correcting him over Howard Herrington's name, she had a feeling it would never come up in conversation again. 'I would never have gone on that stupid date if I hadn't been so desperately unhappy,' she said. 'I was so jealous of you with that model.'

'Maya,' he said, holding her from him again, his expression sombre once more. 'You must believe me when I say I never had anything intimate to do with that woman. She was so vacuous and vain it made me long to be with you again. It's made me realise how wrong it was to make you give up your career. No wonder you were frustrated and bored. You're an intelligent young woman with so much to offer.'

'You didn't make me give up my career,' she said. 'I just thought that's what you and your family expected me to do.'

'I know, which amounts to the same thing,' he said. 'I want you to be fulfilled and happy, *cara*. If you want to teach, then that is fine by me. I will do whatever I can to facilitate your career; just promise not to leave me again.'

Maya smiled again as he brought her close. 'I'm not going anywhere just yet,' she said on a contented sigh. 'I'm quite happy right where I am.'

Five and a half months later...

Maya looked down at the tiny squirming, squalling bundle in her arms and felt her heart swell so much she was sure her chest would not be able to contain it. It was such a miracle to be holding her child. Although he had been in a bit of rush to get into the world, he was absolutely perfect; all his fingers and toes were in place and his little nose and that stubborn chin that looked so much like his father's made her smile every time she looked at it. He had a decent pair of lungs on him too; from the moment he was born he had not stopped letting everyone know he was here at last.

Giorgio was still wiping the tears from his eyes from watching as Maya had so bravely delivered his son into the world. He had cut the cord himself and knew he would never forget the moment when he saw that dark little head appear just before his son's wizened and bloodied body followed in a rush.

'Can you believe it?' Maya said, grinning up at him proudly.

He shook his head, still too choked up to speak; but he reached for her free hand and squeezed it tightly.

'What are we going to call him?' she said, looking back down at the baby, who had finally settled against her breast, suckling hungrily.

Giorgio cleared his throat. 'We didn't get around to discussing names,' he said. 'This poor little man hasn't got a stitch of clothing until I go out and buy some for him.'

Maya looked up at him sheepishly. 'Actually…I did buy a couple of things last week,' she said. 'Bronte took me shopping and I just couldn't resist it. She was buying stuff for Ella and her baby and I wanted to join in.'

Giorgio brushed the sweaty hair off her forehead lovingly. 'So you were a little more confident towards the end than you were letting on?'

'I was confident you would love and support me, no matter what,' she said softly.

He pressed a gentle kiss to her mouth. 'The baby is a bonus, *cara*,' he said, 'a beautiful, precious bonus to a relationship that is worth more to me than all the money in the world.'

'I love you,' she said, blinking back tears of joy.

He smiled and blotted her tears with the pads of his thumbs. 'I love you too, more than words can say. I will never stop loving you.'

The baby gave a little grizzle as he lost suction. Maya

gently eased him back in place before she looked back up at Giorgio. 'So, what do we call him?' she asked. 'Do you have any suggestions?'

Giorgio touched his finger to the tiny reddened cheek of his son. 'How about Matteo?' he said.

'Mmm, I really like that,' Maya said. 'What does it mean?'

'It means gift from God,' he said, and smiled as his gaze meshed with hers over the tiny precious bundle of their surprise baby.

MILLS & BOON®

DECEMBER 2010 HARDBACK TITLES

ROMANCE

Naive Bride, Defiant Wife	Lynne Graham
Nicolo: The Powerful Sicilian	Sandra Marton
Stranded, Seduced...Pregnant	Kim Lawrence
Shock: One-Night Heir	Melanie Milburne
Innocent Virgin, Wild Surrender	Anne Mather
Her Last Night of Innocence	India Grey
Captured and Crowned	Janette Kenny
Buttoned-Up Secretary, British Boss	Susanne James
Surf, Sea and a Sexy Stranger	Heidi Rice
Wild Nights with her Wicked Boss	Nicola Marsh
Mistletoe and the Lost Stiletto	Liz Fielding
Rescued by his Christmas Angel	Cara Colter
Angel of Smoky Hollow	Barbara McMahon
Christmas at Candlebark Farm	Michelle Douglas
The Cinderella Bride	Barbara Wallace
Single Father, Surprise Prince!	Raye Morgan
A Christmas Knight	Kate Hardy
The Nurse Who Saved Christmas	Janice Lynn

HISTORICAL

Lady Arabella's Scandalous Marriage	Carole Mortimer
Dangerous Lord, Seductive Miss	Mary Brendan
Bound to the Barbarian	Carol Townend
Bought: The Penniless Lady	Deborah Hale

MEDICAL™

St Piran's: The Wedding of The Year	Caroline Anderson
St Piran's: Rescuing Pregnant Cinderella	Carol Marinelli
The Midwife's Christmas Miracle	Jennifer Taylor
The Doctor's Society Sweetheart	Lucy Clark

MILLS & BOON

DECEMBER 2010 LARGE PRINT TITLES

ROMANCE

The Pregnancy Shock — Lynne Graham
Falco: The Dark Guardian — Sandra Marton
One Night...Nine-Month Scandal — Sarah Morgan
The Last Kolovsky Playboy — Carol Marinelli
Doorstep Twins — Rebecca Winters
The Cowboy's Adopted Daughter — Patricia Thayer
SOS: Convenient Husband Required — Liz Fielding
Winning a Groom in 10 Dates — Cara Colter

HISTORICAL

Rake Beyond Redemption — Anne O'Brien
A Thoroughly Compromised Lady — Bronwyn Scott
In the Master's Bed — Blythe Gifford
Bought: The Penniless Lady — Deborah Hale

MEDICAL™

The Midwife and the Millionaire — Fiona McArthur
From Single Mum to Lady — Judy Campbell
Knight on the Children's Ward — Carol Marinelli
Children's Doctor, Shy Nurse — Molly Evans
Hawaiian Sunset, Dream Proposal — Joanna Neil
Rescued: Mother and Baby — Anne Fraser

MILLS & BOON

JANUARY 2011 HARDBACK TITLES

ROMANCE

Hidden Mistress, Public Wife	Emma Darcy
Jordan St Claire: Dark and Dangerous	Carole Mortimer
The Forbidden Innocent	Sharon Kendrick
Bound to the Greek	Kate Hewitt
The Secretary's Scandalous Secret	Cathy Williams
Ruthless Boss, Dream Baby	Susan Stephens
Prince Voronov's Virgin	Lynn Raye Harris
Mistress, Mother...Wife?	Maggie Cox
With This Fling...	Kelly Hunter
Girls' Guide to Flirting with Danger	Kimberly Lang
Wealthy Australian, Secret Son	Margaret Way
A Winter Proposal	Lucy Gordon
His Diamond Bride	Lucy Gordon
Surprise: Outback Proposal	Jennie Adams
Juggling Briefcase & Baby	Jessica Hart
Deserted Island, Dreamy Ex!	Nicola Marsh
Rescued by the Dreamy Doc	Amy Andrews
Navy Officer to Family Man	Emily Forbes

HISTORICAL

Lady Folbroke's Delicious Deception	Christine Merrill
Breaking the Governess's Rules	Michelle Styles
Her Dark and Dangerous Lord	Anne Herries
How To Marry a Rake	Deb Marlowe

MEDICAL™

Sheikh, Children's Doctor...Husband	Meredith Webber
Six-Week Marriage Miracle	Jessica Matthews
St Piran's: Italian Surgeon, Forbidden Bride	Margaret McDonagh
The Baby Who Stole the Doctor's Heart	Dianne Drake

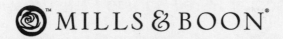

MILLS & BOON

JANUARY 2011 LARGE PRINT TITLES

ROMANCE

A Stormy Greek Marriage	Lynne Graham
Unworldly Secretary, Untamed Greek	Kim Lawrence
The Sabbides Secret Baby	Jacqueline Baird
The Undoing of de Luca	Kate Hewitt
Cattle Baron Needs a Bride	Margaret Way
Passionate Chef, Ice Queen Boss	Jennie Adams
Sparks Fly with Mr Mayor	Teresa Carpenter
Rescued in a Wedding Dress	Cara Colter

HISTORICAL

Vicar's Daughter to Viscount's Lady	Louise Allen
Chivalrous Rake, Scandalous Lady	Mary Brendan
The Lord's Forced Bride	Anne Herries
Wanted: Mail-Order Mistress	Deborah Hale

MEDICAL™

Dare She Date the Dreamy Doc?	Sarah Morgan
Dr Drop-Dead Gorgeous	Emily Forbes
Her Brooding Italian Surgeon	Fiona Lowe
A Father for Baby Rose	Margaret Barker
Neurosurgeon . . . and Mum!	Kate Hardy
Wedding in Darling Downs	Leah Martyn